The Roy
Roy

A brand-new duet by Ally Blake!

It's the day of the royal wedding of Prince
Alessandro Hugo Giordano and Sadie Gray. All of
Vallemont are in attendance...except the bride!

With a media storm raging around them, runaway
princess-to-be Sadie is helped by wedding guest
Will, while jilted Prince Hugo heads to Australia,
where he meets tantalizingly unsuitable Amber.

Will Sadie and Hugo find their happily-ever-afters?
And will Vallemont get the wedding it's been
waiting for?

Find out more in Sadie's story
Rescuing the Royal Runaway Bride

And don't miss Hugo's story
Amber and the Rogue Prince

Both available now!

Amber gave him a look. A look that connected them.

It was the first time they'd spoken with any sense about the fact that they were going to have a child together.

This woman, Hugo thought. His deep subconscious added, *Do not let her slip away, or I will never forgive you.*

But he was about to become the sovereign ruler of a country. His only choice in the matter was to leave emotion out of it, to make her an offer she couldn't refuse.

"Amber," he said.

Hearing the serious note in his voice, her laughter dried up. "Yes, Hugo."

"A week ago I was fifth in line to the throne. In a few days I will return home to be crowned the sovereign prince of Vallemont."

Amber's hand slipped from her hip to her belly.

"There's a strong chance I'm wrong, but I have a feeling that I know where you are going with this. And I think you should stop now. Before either of us says something we can't take back."

"Marry me."

Amber and the Rogue Prince

Ally Blake

HARLEQUIN®ROMANCE

Recycling programs
for this product may
not exist in your area.

ISBN-13: 978-1-335-13515-5

Amber and the Rogue Prince

First North American publication 2018

Printed in U.S.A.

www.Harlequin.com

Australian author **Ally Blake** loves reading and strong coffee, porch swings and dappled sunshine, beautiful notebooks and soft, dark pencils. Her inquisitive, rambunctious, spectacular children are her exquisite delights. And she adores writing love stories so much she'd write them even if nobody else read them. No wonder, then, having sold over four million copies of her romance novels worldwide, Ally is living her bliss. Find out more about Ally's books at allyblake.com.

Books by Ally Blake

Harlequin Romance

The Royals of Vallemont

Rescuing the Royal Runaway Bride

Billionaire on Her Doorstep
Millionaire to the Rescue
Falling for the Rebel Heir
Hired: The Boss's Bride
Dating the Rebel Tycoon
Millionaire Dad's SOS

Harlequin KISS

The Rules of Engagement
Faking It to Making It
The Dance Off
Her Hottest Summer Yet

Visit the Author Profile page
at Harlequin.com for more titles.

For all the women dreaming about their next chapters.

And Bec, who leaped into hers with enthusiasm, fortitude, grace, humor and style, taking her first steps alongside me, and naming Ned the dog along the way.

**Praise for
Ally Blake**

"Now I'm used to being entertained by Ally Blake's wit, enjoying her young quirky heroines and drooling over her dark, brooding heroes. But this book stuck inside me somehow."

—*Goodreads* on *Millionaire Dad's SOS*

CHAPTER ONE

AMBER PLONKED HERSELF onto the rickety stairs out front of the shack hovering on the edge of Serenity Hill. Stretching her arms over her head, she blinked sleepily at the view.

A misty glow slithered over the acres of wild lavender carpeting the hillside. The first hint of morning sun peeked between the hilly mounds beyond, creating a starburst of gold on the horizon and making silhouettes of the willows meandering along the banks of Serenity Creek below.

"Could do with some rain," said Amber. "That said, can't we always?"

Ned stared fondly up at her from his mismatched eyes. She gave the mottled fur behind his good ear a thorough rub.

Then, nabbing her bright yellow gumboots, Amber tugged them on over faded pyjama bottoms. She rubbed a smudge of mud from one of the bees that Sunflower—who lived in the bright purple caravan up on the hill—had painted on them for her. Then she twirled her heavy hair into a low bun and ducked her head into her fencing-style veil. Last came elasticised gloves, then, finally ready, she pushed herself to her feet.

"You ready?"

Ned answered with a wag of his tail.

"Then let's do this."

But Amber only made it down one more step before she spied Sunflower hustling down the hill behind the shack towards her.

With her fluffy strawberry-blonde hair and pixie face, her feet bare beneath her long paisley skirt, Sunflower looked as if she'd fallen to earth on a sunbeam. But like everyone in Serenity she'd come in search of sanctuary.

Amber pulled off her veil and tucked it under her arm before wiping the dislodged strands of hair from her eyes. Not used to seeing anyone else out and about this early, Amber called out, "Everything okay?"

Sunflower waved a hand while she caught her breath. "I have news."

"For you to be out from under your blanket this early it must be pretty good news."

The look Sunflower shot her was thick with meaning.

"Not so good, then."

Sunflower shielded her face against the rising sun and said, "I'm actually not sure. The news is they've opened up the Big House."

Amber glanced up the hill, even though Hinterland House—the big, deserted, Tuscan-style villa that everyone in the area simply referred to as the Big House—was perched too far over the other side to be seen.

"Grim mentioned seeing smoke coming from the chimney a couple of weeks back. But considering Grim lives in a cloud of smoke, I ignored it. Then Daphne claimed she saw sheets on the clothesline and I began to wonder. Last night, when he was taking one of his wanders, my Johnno saw a fancy black car barrelling up the drive and pulling into the garage." She paused for effect, then announced, "It seems the family is back."

"What family? The way the place was always kept so well-tended I'd figured it was a tax write-off for some overseas conglomerate."

"Oh, no," said Sunflower, her eyes now dancing. "It belongs to the Van Halprins. A family as famous for their money and power as their terrible bad luck. As the story goes, they all died off, in one tragic manner after another, until only one remained—the youngest daughter, Anna, who was very beautiful. Twenty-one and all alone in that big house—the townspeople feared what might become of her. Then, in a fairy-tale ending, she married a prince from some far-off land and the place has been barren ever since."

"And now this fairy-tale princess is back?"

Sunflower shook her head, her eyes sparking. "The person my Johnno saw driving the car was a man. City haircut. Deadly handsome. They say it's *him*."

Amber knew she was meant to say, *Him who?* but her throat had gone dry. Her earlier frisson of concern now bore the hallmarks of fully fledged anxiety: sweaty palms; ringing in her ears; a strong desire to run inside and bar the door.

But the door to her shack was barely holding onto its hinges as it was, so what would be the point?

Oblivious, sweet Sunflower went on. "It *has* to be Anna's son! Anna's *royal* son. Prince Alessandro Giordano himself."

Not one to follow that kind of thing, Amber didn't know Prince Alessandro from Prince Charming.

Only, she had an awful feeling she did.

"Don't you see?" Sunflower went on. "As heir to the Van Halprin estate, Prince Alessandro owns Hinterland House, which means he also owns pretty much every bit of land you can see. From one side of the hill to the other, from the river to the township. Including the land you and I are standing on."

Amber found she had to swallow before asking, "Whoa. Back up a little. I assumed the commune owned this land. Or that the township simply let them stay." So deeply grateful had she been for a place to stay, she'd never thought to ask. "Are you saying that this *Prince* owns Serenity Hill?"

Sunflower nodded slowly. "And there are more rumours."

There were always rumours. Especially in a town this size. Having had parents whose chief personality trait was "being deeply involved", Amber had developed a sincere lack of interest in knowing other people's business.

Sunflower said, "Apparently a man fitting that description—tall, citified, handsome, *and* with an accent—has been seen meeting with the town council. And the only reason for an outsider to meet with the council is—"

"Town planning."

The wind had picked up, creating eerie paths through the field of lavender. And despite the sun lifting into the air, Amber shivered. She wriggled her toes in her gumboots in order to keep the blood flowing.

Unlike some of the old-timers living in tents, wigwams, caravans and Kombi vans up the hill, Amber was a relative newcomer to Serenity. But, while her history of the area was sketchy, her experience with the law was sharp and clear.

"The commune has been occupying this land for years. Decades, right? Long enough to build structures. To hook in plumbing. Electricity. To have signs pointing the way. It's even noted as a point of interest on the tourist map. Surely that gives us rights."

Sunflower blinked. "Rights?"

Before Amber could take the thought further, something banged inside her shack. Both women turned to see what it was. Amber took a subtle step back up onto the porch.

"Probably Ned demanding breakfast."

Sunflower backed away. "Of course. I'm off to spread the news to the rest of the morning folk. See what else we can unearth. Feel free to fill everyone in yourself. Fire-pit meeting tonight. At sunset."

Another bang came from inside Amber's shack. She took another step nearer her front door. Said, "You bet. See you then. I'd better check on Ned."

Of course, at that moment Ned came running out of the fields below, purple flowers caught in his fur.

Amber madly ushered Ned inside the shack, then yanked the door shut behind her before leaning against it, holding the doorknob tight.

In the quiet her heart thumped against her ribs.

All she had to do was lean forward to see past the cupboard-cum-kitchen wall and into her small bedroom. To spot the crumpled sheets. The colourful crocheted blanket kicked into a pile on the floor.

And the masculine shape of the stranger in her bed.

A chop of sun-kissed hair slid over one eye. Broad shoulders lifted and fell as he breathed. The profile cast against her pillow was achingly handsome. Even now. Even with the indignation building inside of her.

To think, she'd only slipped out from under the warm, heavy weight of his arm ten minutes before, smiling at what a deep sleeper he was. And the reason why.

He'd said his name was Hugo. And she'd believed him.

That particular something in his eyes—directness, authority, unflappability—had allowed her the rare luxury of taking everything he'd said at face value. No doubt the foreign accent had helped too. Not only was it devastatingly sexy, but it also meant he was a tourist, just passing through. There was no point worrying too much about details when their dalliance was only ever going to be short-term.

And yet, it sounded like the man she'd just indulged in a clandestine three-week affair with was none other than Prince Alessandro Giordano—and he was also known as the owner of the land on which she and her friends lived illegally!

Three weeks earlier...

Amber breathed in the scent of lavender as she looked out over Serenity Hill.

There had been a chill in the air that morning. Like the blast of an open fridge door on a hot summer's day.

It was the sign she had been waiting for. Time to harvest her bumper honey crop for the year. Collect at the right time and the honey would be ripe, sweet, in its prime. Leave it much longer and the colony would start eating the wares or moving it lower into the hive, making it near impossible to collect.

By late afternoon there was no need for the smoker. Warmth had settled over the valley and crept up onto the hills, meaning the honey would be warm, running easily, and the bees would be calm.

Dolled up in her veil, overalls and gloves, gumboots slapping against the stairs, she realised Ned was not at her side. No point whistling for him—he was nearly deaf.

She tipped up onto her toes to see if she could spy his fluffy tail cutting through the field. No luck. Maybe he'd headed up the hill to visit the others. But that wasn't like him. They knew better than to feed him scraps. Amber had made it clear that he was her responsibility, nobody else's. That in taking him on she wouldn't put undue pressure on the commune's resources.

About to give up and head off alone, she saw him by the pair of trees down the hill, watching the hammock slung between them with great interest.

As Amber neared she realised why.

A stranger in fact was lying therein. Asleep.

Not just a stranger…a man. A *long* man. Longer than the hammock, his big feet poking out of the end. His T-shirt had twisted to cling to a sculpted chest. The bottom edge lifted to reveal a tanned stomach, and a dark arrow of hair leading to…jeans that left little to the imagination.

Even in sleep he was riveting. Deep-set eyes beneath dashing, slashing brows, and overlong hair that fell across a brow furrowed as if he was dreaming important dreams. The rest of his face was rough-hewn, but handsome with it—a stubble-shadowed jaw and cheeks that appeared carved from rock. A veritable modern-day Viking.

Not from around here, or she'd have noticed. A tourist, then. Not the seasonal fruit-picking kind. Or the type who came to Serenity looking for enlightenment. Or absolution. His clothes were too nice. His aura too crisp. But people didn't just happen to pass through Serenity. They came with a purpose. So what was his?

Her gaze running over every inch of him as if she was committing him to memory, Amber realised with excruciating discomfort just how long she'd been living in this patch of pretty wilderness dotted with leisurely artisans and gentle hippies, none of whom had made her nerves twang. Not like this.

She swallowed the thirst pooling in her cheeks and reached out for Ned.

Ned looked at her with his contented face.

"What are you grinning at?"

Forgetting the fact that in all likelihood the stranger was not as deaf as Ned, Amber hadn't thought to lower her voice.

The stranger sprang to sitting as if he were spring-loaded. His feet hit the ground, his hands gripping the edges of the hammock, the muscles of his arms bunching as the hammock threatened to swing out from under him.

He was even bigger sitting up. Well over six feet. Strong with it. Yet Amber felt compelled to stay. To watch. To wait.

A few beats later, the stranger shook his hair from his eyes before palming the heels of his hands deep into the sockets. With a heavy breath he dropped his hands, opened his eyes, took one look at Amber and leapt out of the hammock so fast he nearly tripped over his own feet.

A string of words poured from his mouth.

Italian? French? Who cared? It was the sexiest sound Amber had ever heard. Raw and deep, it scraped against her insides like a long, slow, rough-tongued lick.

Ned loved it too, what little he could hear of it. He bounded to his feet and ran around in a circle, barking at the sky.

The stranger looked over his shoulder, then back at Amber. He looked down at Ned, then back at her again. This time his gaze caught. And stayed. A beat slunk by in which deep breaths were hard to come by.

Then, in lightly accented English, "Please tell me you come in peace."

She reached up and slowly pulled her bee-keeping hat and veil from her head. As usual, the mesh caught on her hair, pulling long blonde strands free of her bun until it fell over her face in a wispy curtain. She tried wiping them away but the heavy glove made it next to impossible.

In the end, she threw her veil to the ground, slid off both gloves and threw them down too. Feeling overheated, she unzipped her overalls, pulling them down to her hips, the arms flapping about her thighs. She fixed her tank top, pushed her hair back off her face, and—hands on hips—stared the stranger down.

The effect somewhat lessened when Ned saw his chance and went for her gloves. He managed to get both, but dropped one about a metre away as he took off into the lavender with the score in his delighted teeth.

Not that the stranger seemed to notice. His eyes never left hers. In fact, they had warmed, distinctly, the edge of a very fine mouth tilting at one side as he took her in.

Flustered, Amber pressed her shoulders back, angled her chin at him and said, "I might ask the same of you."

"Me?" He stretched his arms overhead, once again revealing his flat, tanned belly, and Amber gritted her teeth as she looked determinedly anywhere else. "I am all about the peace."

"Well, next time keep your peace far from my hammock. *Capiche?*"

"If I said I really needed a nap at the exact moment I came upon it, would that help?" One side of his mouth kicked up, and her tummy tumbled over on itself in response.

"What do you think?" she deadpanned.

"I think perhaps not," he mumbled, running a hand through his hair. It was a little rumpled from sleep on one side. He wore it well.

He took a step her way, and Amber took an equal step back, which was ridiculous. If she screamed, a dozen hippies would rush down the hill to check on her. Well, maybe not rush. Amble with intent.

She pressed her gumboots into the ground. It wasn't concern for her safety that had her on edge. It was concern for her hazy judgement.

He stepped sideways, picked up the glove Ned had dropped and ran his thumb over the honeycomb stitching. "How about if I said I tripped and fell into the hammock, knocking myself out?"

"I'd think you were an idiot."

A smile tugging at the corner of that mouth, he looked out over the lavender, all the while taking a step closer to her. "Then here's the unvarnished truth: a wicked witch lured me here with a peach. I took one bite and fell into a deep sleep."

As punctuation, he held out her glove. Naturally, she reached out to take it. Only he did not let go, capturing her gaze right along with it.

His eyes were a deep, intelligent hazel, his mouth on the constant verge of a smile. The fact that his nose appeared to have been broken at some time only added to his stunning good looks.

"It was an apple," said Amber, her voice breaking on the last syllable.

"Hmm?" he said, gently letting the glove go.

"Sleeping Beauty was felled by an apple."

Again with the devastating half-smile. "Wasn't that Eve with the apple? Tempting poor Adam."

"Forbidden fruit. No mention of an apple, specifically."

"Right. I stand corrected."

At some point in the past few minutes, the sun had begun to set, stretching shadows over the stranger's arresting face.

But it was the words that had her transfixed. The locals were so earnest she couldn't remember the last time she'd indulged in spicy banter. It felt good. Really good. Like slipping into a freshly made bed after a long day on her feet.

"Who are you?" she asked, the desire to know far too obvious in her tone.

He held out a hand. "Hugo. And you are?"

Feeling as if she was about to step off a cliff, she took his hand. His fingers were long and strong. His grip dry and warm. The tingle that zapped up her arm had her shaking once and letting go.

"Amber."

"It's a very great pleasure to meet you, Amber."

"I'll bet."

At that he laughed.

The sound tumbling about inside her belly made her feel empty. Hungry. She breathed through it. "Wicked witch or no, this is private property, so you'd best get moving on. It doesn't get fully dark for another hour. If you walk with pace you'll make it to the village in time. There you'll find somewhere else to sleep."

The man slid his hands into his pockets and rocked back on his heels, going nowhere.

Amber crossed her arms and shook her head at the guy. But he only smiled back, the directness in his eyes telling her she wasn't the only one having an "interested at first sight" moment. She rolled her eyes, turned on her heel and beckoned to him over her shoulder.

"Come on, then, Hugo. This way."

CHAPTER TWO

HUGO TWISTED AND stretched, enjoying the creaks and cracks of muscles well-used.

Still half-asleep, he couldn't be sure if the images skirting the edges of his brain were real, or the remnants of a very good dream. Then slowly, like drops of mercury melting together, he recalled slippery limbs sliding over each other. Warmth easing towards heat. Sighs, laughter, a gasp.

No dream. Just Amber.

A bump to the bed echoed through him, as if it wasn't the first.

He dragged his eyes open, battling the sharp morning sunshine, to find Amber no longer tucked into his side. Instead, she stood by the other side of her bed, glaring at him.

And he found himself riding a wave of déjà-vu.

The first time he'd laid eyes on her she'd worn the white veiled hat and the long, chunky gloves, the bulky overalls and those wild yellow boots. She'd looked like something from a nineteen-fifties space comic. Then she'd stripped down in front of him, all sun-browned shoulders, wildly tangled lashes over whisky-brown bedroom eyes, full lips, her long hair a halo of honeyed gold falling halfway down her back.

The difference this time: her lips were pursed. Her hands white-knuckled on her hips. And her narrowed eyes shot daggers his way.

That didn't stop him from weighing up the likelihood of dragging her back to bed. He deemed the chances slim.

Brought up never to readily surrender the advantage of position, Hugo sat up, the sheet dragging with him. His feet curled as they hit the rough wooden floor. Then he pulled himself to standing.

Amber's gaze flickered to his bare chest and she sucked in a sharp breath. The chances looked slightly more promising.

But then her arm lifted, one pointed finger aimed towards her front door, and she said, "Get out."

"Excuse me?"

"I said, get out. Do you not understand what that means? Were you raised by wolves?"

"Nannies. Mostly."

"Of course you were. Get out of my bed. Get out of my shack. Now."

Hugo ran both hands over his face, hard and fast. Better to be fully awake for this. "Start at the beginning. You're not making any sense."

"Then look at my face. Look deep into my eyes

so that you see I am serious. I want you to get out."

Well, this was new. Her voice rose with each word, rare emotion tinging her words. She was genuinely upset.

"I will go. Of course. If that's what you want. Look, I'm already out of your bed." The sheet at his hips slipped as he reached up to scratch his chest.

Her tongue darted out to wet her lips, which alleviated his concern, at least a little.

"In the spirit of fair play, I deserve to know why. What has changed in the world since you fell asleep while trying to convince me that honey was better than peanut butter?"

Her hand dropped, just a fraction. Then she regrouped, pointing her finger towards the door with renewed conviction. "Nothing has changed. Not a single thing. Apart from the fact that I now know who you really are."

Time stood still for the merest fraction of a second, but when it resumed, everything seemed to sit a little off from where it had before.

He nodded, dropped the sheet back onto the bed and ambled over to the metal chair in the corner to gather his clothes. His underwear was nowhere to be seen, and, not about to go searching, he went commando, pulling on his jeans, taking care with the fly.

He'd known their liaison would end. They both had. That had been the underlying beauty of it.

In the first few days it had been diverting, watching things unfold from a safe mental distance. Distance was his usual state of being and Amber had seemed glad of it. The guiltless pleasure, the ease of transaction, the lack of desire on both sides to pry deeper than what the other might like for lunch had led to a beautifully contained affair.

Somehow, in all the hazy sunshine, with the cicadas a constant background hum, the clear edges of their association had begun to blur…until he'd found reasons to come to her earlier, to stay longer. They'd fallen into a rhythm of days lit bright and nights lost to exquisite, immoderate pleasure and murmured nothings in the dark.

As he pushed one arm through his shirt, then the other, he no longer felt distant. The dissatisfaction he felt was real.

But only a fool would have expected the halcyon days to remain that way—like a bug trapped in amber. So to speak. And Hugo was no fool.

"Is that it?" Amber's words hit his back like bullets. "You don't have anything to say for yourself?"

He patted his jeans pockets in search of his wallet, phone, keys—then remembered he didn't carry any. Not here. So he snapped the top button before looking up at her. "What would you like me to say, Amber?"

"I don't know, that I'm acting crazy? That I've been duped—by someone other than you, I mean. That it's not true."

She looked so incorruptible, like a force of nature. But something he'd learned in his month in this part of the world—nobody came to Serenity without a good reason. Or a bad one.

He opened his mouth to call her on it, but he stopped himself in time.

He'd never known someone to wear their absoluteness like a badge of honour the way she did. The moment she'd decided to let him into her house she'd decided to let him into her bed. No coquettish equivocation. Only firm decision.

This was the first time he'd seen it waver. Enough for him to take heed. To hold out his hands in conciliation. "I never lied to you, Amber. I am Hugo to my friends, my closest family."

"To everyone else?"

"I am Prince Alessandro Hugo Giordano, sixth in line to the principality of Vallemont."

The quiet that followed his statement wasn't new. The rare times Hugo found himself in a conversation with someone who wasn't aware of who he was, what he was worth, and who his relatives were, it was clear when the penny dropped.

Though this might have been the first time he

was half-dressed when that realisation occurred, he thought ruefully.

A hippy beekeeper on the Central Coast of Australia had not been in the plan, meaning it was taking him a little longer to decide upon the appropriate protocol with which to navigate this moment.

Meanwhile, Amber's nostrils flared, fury dancing behind her bedroom eyes. He imagined she was finding it hard not to climb over the bed and tackle him. As unmoved by convention as she was, she could do it too.

For a man whose entire life had been ruled by ritual, no wonder she'd been impossible to resist.

"Wait," he said. "Fifth. I'm fifth in line. My uncle's recently abdicated all rights and moved to California to produce movies. Not that it matters. I am a prince in name only. I will never rule."

She blinked and it was enough to snap her from her red haze. "I don't give a flying hoot if you are set to be Master of the Universe. Don't even think about turning us out on our ears."

"Excuse me?"

"These people are special. The community needs this place. The commune is Serenity's heart. If you mess with that you will kill it dead."

That was what had her so het up? Not *who* he was, but the plans he had for this land?

What the hell had she found out? And how?

This wasn't his first rodeo. He'd been discreet. Painstakingly so. Who had talked?

He did up a couple of quick buttons on his shirt before re-rolling the sleeves to his elbows. Then he moved slowly around the bed, hands out, palms up.

"Amber, until this point in time, we have been having a nice time together. I'd go so far as to say very nice. With that in mind, I suggest we sit down, have a cup of coffee and discuss any concerns you might have."

He could still fix this.

"I don't want to discuss anything with you. I just want you to tell me, right here, right now, if the rumours are true."

"Which rumours might they be, exactly?"

"That you have been meeting with the local town council. Discussing plans…development plans that may or may not put the commune in danger."

"Would that be such a bad thing?"

Emotion flickered behind her eyes. Deep, frantic, fierce. "Yes," she managed. "It would be a terrible thing."

"Look at this place, Amber. It's falling down around your ears."

"Not every home has to be a castle."

Touché. "And yet if you have the chance to sleep somewhere that doesn't whistle, drip, or threaten to fall down the hill every time you step onto the porch, it's worth considering."

"My sleeping arrangements are none of your business."

"They became my business when I began sleeping here too."

"Lucky for you that is not a problem you'll have to face again."

Hugo breathed out hard, while emotion darted and flashed behind her big brown eyes. With the tension sparking in the air between them, it was all he could do to keep from going to her and letting the slow burn of her fill the empty places inside.

"Tell me, right now, if we have made incorrect assumptions. Are you planning on developing the land? Should we be concerned?"

A muscle ticked beneath his eye. And she took it for the admission it was.

Amber slumped onto the corner of the bed, her face falling into her hands. "This can't be happening."

"I hope you understand that until anything is concrete I can't discuss the details."

She looked up at him, beseeching. "Understand? I don't understand any of this. Like why, if you are so offended by my home, you kept coming back. Was I reconnaissance? Were you hoping to create an ally in your devious plans?"

"Of course not, Amber." Hugo's stomach dropped and he came around the bed, crouching before her. "Amber, you know why I came back. And back. And back. For the same reason you took me in."

He lifted a hand and closed it around hers. Her soft brown eyes begged him to stop. Heat sat high and pink on her cheeks. Her wild waves of hair caught on a breeze coming through one of the many cracks in the woebegone shack in which she lived.

Then her fingers softened as she curled them into his.

A moment later, she whipped her hand away and gave him a shove that had him rocking onto his backside with a thump that shook the foundations, raining dust over his head as she scrambled over him and into clear space.

As he cleared the dust from his hair, his eyes, Hugo wondered how his life had come to this.

The downward spiral had begun several months earlier when he'd agreed to his uncle's sovereign command to enter into a marriage of convenience. His former fiancée—and long-time best friend— Sadie, had come to her senses and fled before they'd said *I do*, bringing about a PR nightmare for the royal family…and freedom for Hugo. The fact that he would likely have gone through with it had been a wake-up call. What had he been thinking? Where was his moral compass? Not that that should be much of a shock—he was his father's son after all.

Afterwards he'd needed to get away. Clear his head. Recalibrate. He'd never have imagined that would lead him away from a life of luxury to camping out in a small, lumpy bed in a country town in the middle of nowhere, Australia, tangled up with a woman he barely knew.

He'd not hidden his position on purpose, she'd simply never asked. Their affair had been lived in the moment, fulfilling basic needs of hunger and sleep and sex while talking about everything from *Game of Thrones* to Eastern philosophy… but nothing truly personal. His family had not come up. Nor, for that matter, had hers. He'd been so grateful to avoid talking about his own that he had given no thought as to why she might also be glad of it. Perhaps he was not the only one for whom that question opened Pandora's box. Either way, after a while, the privacy had felt like a true luxury.

"I need you to leave, Hugo," said Amber, yanking him back to the present, only this time she added, "Please."

It was enough for Hugo to push to standing. He looked around the small, dilapidated room, but he'd left nothing behind bar the impression of his head on the pillow. It didn't seem like enough.

Too late to rectify that now, he turned to walk out.

"Wait," she called, grabbing him by the arm. Before he even had the chance to feel relief she pressed past him and headed out onto her wonky porch, causing the area around her shack to tremble in response.

Ned nuzzled against his hand. And Hugo lost his fingers in the dog's soft fur, taking a moment to work out a burr.

"All clear," Amber called.

"Wouldn't want your friends to know you've been harbouring the enemy."

She glanced back at him, the morning sun turning her hair to gold, her eyes to fire. When she saw Ned at his side her mouth pursed. "Away," she called. But Ned didn't move, whether because of his deafness or his obstinacy. She clicked her fingers and with a *harumph* the dog jogged to her side.

He joined them on the porch. The old wood creaked and groaned. A handmade wooden wind chime pealed prettily in the morning breeze.

"Is that why you came to Serenity?"

Now, there was a question. One she might have thought to ask at any point during the last few weeks if she'd had a care to know anything at all about the man she'd been sleeping with. "You really want to know what I came to Serenity hoping to find?"

She only nodded mutely.

"Absolution. How about you?"

She snapped her mouth shut tight.

He raised an eyebrow. *Now, what do you have to say about that?*

Nothing, it seemed. He'd finally managed to render Amber speechless.

With that, Hugo left her there in her bright yellow gumboots, her tank top clinging to her lovely body, her hair a wild, sexy mess. He jogged down the steps and headed down the hill, past the hammock, through the field of lavender to the small dead-end dirt road on which he'd parked his car.

The urge to look back was acute but he kept his cool. Because he had the feeling that it wouldn't be the last he saw of Amber.

She might be done with him, but he wasn't done with Serenity. For he did indeed have plans for his mother's ancestral home—plans which had him excited for the first time since the debacle of the wedding that never was. He might even go so far as to say they excited him more than any other development he had ever actualised.

For Hugo was renowned for taking underused or overlooked tracts of land that others would deem too remote or too challenging, and turning them into stunning holiday playgrounds for diplomats, royalty, the rich and famous, and families alike. His series of Vallemontian resorts—including a palatial masterpiece tucked into the side of Mont Enchante and an award-winning titan overlooking Lake Glace—had been a revelation for the local economy, making him invaluable to his uncle in terms of commerce if not in terms of the line of succession.

But this one, this place…it would be all his.

When he reached the bottom of the lavender field he did look back, Amber's shack and the rest of the commune relegated to glimpses of purple and red and orange obscured by copses of gum trees.

He'd keep the natural landscape as much as possible, but the caravans, tents and shanties would of course have to go to make way for the bungalows, tennis courts, lagoon-style pool and a peach grove where Amber's shack now wobbled.

Hugo wasn't some monstrous land baron. With the council's help, he would assist them in their relocation. Help them find safer places to live.

And he would create something beautiful, something lasting, something personal to break the cycle of tragedy in his mother's family.

He would make his very personal mark on the world without trading on his family name, a constant reminder of the top job for which he and his heirs would only ever be back-ups.

Amber would just have to lump it.

* * *

Serenity's Town Hall was packed to the rafters, with people lining the walls and spilling out through the open doors. It was late enough that young ones would normally be home in bed, but nobody was missing this meeting, so they sat in messy rows on the floor at the front, making occasional mad dashes across the stage, followed by their harassed parents.

There was only one reason for the big turnout: the news had spread. Nothing this momentous had happened in Serenity since Anna had been swept away to an exotic foreign land.

Amber slumped on her bench in the third row, her legs jiggling, her thumbs dancing over her fingertips. There was a good portion of the commune lined up beside her, including Sunflower, who was humming happily despite the cacophony of white noise, and Johnno, who was staring out into space.

Only, Amber wasn't here in the hope of spotting the exotic stranger. She'd seen enough of him already, from the scar above his right eyebrow to the birthmark on the base of his left big toe—and everything in between. She shifted on her seat and cleared her throat.

She was here in case the Hinterland House plans—whatever they might be—were on the agenda in the hope she could see with her own eyes as someone shouted it down. Then Hugo would leave and things could go back to normal. Or as normal as things ever got in Serenity.

Someone, but not her.

It hadn't passed her by that her parents would have loved this kind of David and Goliath fight—though nobody would have mistaken them for David in their Gucci suits and Mercedes four-wheel drives. It made them great lawyers, but terrible parents.

How could they be expected to nurse a "difficult" baby when there was so much injustice to stamp down? Enough that Australia's most infamous human rights lawyers put the care of their only child into the hands of daycare and night nannies from six weeks of age. Their work was far too important for them to abide the distraction.

The smack of a gavel split the silence and Amber flinched, reminded of the number of courtrooms she'd been in as a child. Well, she didn't have the mental space to think about her parents today. Or ever, if at all possible. She sat taller, stopped her nervous fidgets and waited.

"Squeeze up," called a voice as someone managed to squash into the end of Amber's row, the rickety wooden bench wobbling as the crowd sardined. When she looked back to the stage, Councillor Paulina Pinkerton—the leader of the seven-member local council—and her cohorts trailed onto the stage then took their seats.

The gavel struck a second time. Amber flinched again. It was a conditioned response, like Pavlov's ruddy dog. The twitters settled to a hush, chairs scratched against the wooden floor, a teenaged boy laughed. Somebody coughed. A baby started to fret. And the town of Serenity held its breath.

"Nice to see so many of you here today. I might choose to think it's because you've heard around the traps how darned interesting our meetings are, but I fear there is some issue that has you all aflutter. So let's get through the necessaries."

The councilwoman swept through the minutes and old business with alacrity. Then she opened the floor.

"Any new business?"

The hum started up again. Whispers, murmurs, the shuffle of bottoms turning on seats. But nobody said a word.

"Fine. Next meeting will be…next Tuesday at— Ms Hartley? Did you have something to add?"

Amber blinked to hear her name being called from the councillors' table, only to realise she was on her feet. Did she have something to add? No! Legally emancipated from her indifferent parents at sixteen in a legal battle that had become a national story in a slow news week, she'd spent her life living like dandelion fluff, flitting from place to place, *not* getting involved.

Until Serenity. Sunflower had taken one look at her empty backpack, her bedraggled state and offered the shack for a night, then another, and somehow she'd found herself stuck in this sweet place, with these kind people, none of whom had a clue what was about to befall them.

This place…it was her sanctuary. And she'd harboured the enemy—however unwittingly. She owed it to them to do whatever it took to protect them.

Damn him. Damn Hugo Prince Whatever-His-Name-Was and his whole crazy family for making her do this.

Amber scooted past the knees blocking her way down the bench. Once she had reached the small rostrum—a literal soapbox attached to a stand fashioned out of a fallen tree, which had been a gift to the town from Johnno, who was a pretty brilliant artist when he was in the right head-space—Amber squared her shoulders, looked each councilman and councilwoman in the eye and prayed her parents would never hear word of what she was about to do.

"Ms Hartley." Councillor Pinkerton gave Amber an encouraging smile. "The floor is yours."

"Thank you. I'll get right to it. I have come to understand that the owners of Hinterland House are back and I believe that they have plans to develop the land. Firstly, I'd like to know if the latter is true, and, if so, I put forward a motion to stop it."

Once she had started, the words poured out of her like water from a busted pipe. Energy surged through the crowd behind her like a snake. It was electric. And she hated it. Because the thrill of the fight was in her veins after all.

"Much of Serenity belongs to the Van Halprins, Ms Hartley, and, apart from the segments bequeathed to the township, they are within their rights to develop that land."

"Into what?"

The councillor paused, clearly thinking through how much she was legally allowed to say, and legally allowed to hold back. "The plans as they are will be up for local consideration soon enough. The Prince plans to build a resort."

Whispers broke out all over the room.

Amber breathed out hard. Sunflower's rumours were one thing, Hugo's indefinite admissions another. But having Councillor Pinkerton admit to as much had Amber feeling sick to the stomach. In fact, she had to breathe for a few seconds in order to keep her stomach from turning over completely.

She glanced over her shoulder and saw Johnno grinning serenely back at her; found Sunflower watching her like a proud sister. Her gaze landed on another dozen members of their collective community—all of whom had come to Serenity in search of acceptance and kindness and peace.

Where would people like them, people like her, go if they had to move on?

She turned back to the front, her heart pumping so hard it seemed to be trying to escape her chest. The room was so still now, even the fretting baby had quieted, meaning her voice made it all the way to the rear of the room and out into the halls, hitting every ear as she said, "I ask that Council accept the inclusive community living on Serenity Hill has been in residence long enough to legally remain. I cry adverse possession."

The murmurs began in earnest. Most asking what the heck adverse possession was.

"For those who do not know the legalese," said Councillor Pinkerton into her microphone, "Ms Hartley is claiming squatter's rights."

At that, the town hall exploded as a hundred conversations began at once. Cheers came from some corners, jeers from others. The fretting baby began to cry in earnest.

The gavel smacked against the wooden table, quieting the crowd somewhat. And this time it rang through Amber like an old bell. Sweet and familiar and pure.

"Thank you, Ms Hartley. Your position has been noted. Does anyone else have anything to say on the matter?"

Amber glanced over her shoulder to find movement at the back of the hall.

A man had stepped into the aisle, a man with overlong hair swept away from his striking face and dark hazel eyes that locked onto Amber. She didn't realise her lungs had stopped functioning until her chest began to ache.

Hugo. But not the Hugo she knew. Not the man in the worn jeans and button-downs who was happy rolling on the ground with Ned, watching her collect honey, or sitting on her stairs staring towards the horizon chewing on a blade of grass.

This was Hugo the Prince. His stark jaw was clean-shaven and he looked dashing in a slick three-piece suit with such bearing, composure and self-assurance he was barely human. Behind him stood a big, hulking bald man in black, watching over him like a hawk.

She hoped no one noticed how hard she clenched her fists.

"Your Highness, good evening, sir," said Councillor Pinkerton, the friendly note of her voice making it clear it was not the first time she'd set eyes on the man.

Hugo's deep voice rang out across the room. "If I may?"

Councillor Pinkerton waved a hurry-up hand. "Up you come, then. State your name for the record. And your purpose."

While Amber had had to climb over a tangle of legs to get to the lectern, the crowd parted for Hugo like the Red Sea.

He slowed as he neared, his head cocking ever so slightly in a private hello.

Amber hated the way her cheeks warmed at the sight of him, her heart thumping against her ribs as if giving the death throes of remembered desire. Nevertheless, she held her ground, waiting until the last moment to give up her position. Then, with an exaggerated bow from the waist, she swooshed out an arm, giving him the floor as she backed away.

Laughter coursed through the crowd.

Hugo's smile eased back, just a fraction. Enough for Amber to know she'd scored a hit.

All's fair, she thought, in love and war. And this was war.

"Councillor Pinkerton," he said, "Council members, good people of Serenity. I thank you for this opportunity to introduce myself to this community."

His hand went to his heart on the last few words, and Amber rolled her eyes.

But the crowd? They were hooked. Straining forward so as not to miss a word spoken in that deep, hypnotic, lilting voice. And he was ramping up the accent. Big time. Playing the dashing foreigner card for all it was worth.

"It has taken me far too long to return to the home of my mother's family, but in the days I have spent wandering the hills and vales your home has come to hold a special place in my heart. And I cannot wait to tell my friends and family about this gem of a place. To invite them here to meet all of you good people. To give the world a taste of Serenity."

Amber rolled her eyes again. But when she looked out over the crowd she saw even members of the commune listening with interest. Including Sunflower, who looked entranced. And then came a smattering of delighted applause.

Enough. Amber marched back up to the rostrum and gave Hugo a shove with her hip, ignoring the wave of heat that rocked through her at his touch. She grabbed the microphone so roughly that the feedback quieted the room.

"Really?" she said, her voice echoing darkly around the room. "*A taste of Serenity...?* It's like a cheesy brochure."

Hugo laughed. And she knew she had surprised him. He licked his lips, swallowing it back, but the light of it lingered in his eyes.

"He," said Amber, pointing an accusing finger towards the Prince, "is *not* one of us. His words might be pretty but his plans are not. And I can't stand to—"

Something lodged in her throat then. Something that felt a lot like a swell of deep emotion, the kind that preceded tears.

Come on! She wasn't a crier! She breathed out hard. And managed to keep her cool.

"It would be a grave injustice to see Serenity lost under the overwhelming influx of tourism that would come by way of a resort. I hope, I *believe*, that you are with me on this point: Serenity's future must be allowed to evolve as it always has—organically."

If Hugo's words had been met with happy claps, Amber's were met with a standing ovation, and a cheer that all but lifted the roof off the place.

The gavel banged several times before Councillor Pinkerton regained control. "Assuming that's all the new business, we will keep further discussion to next week's town meeting. Date and time as mentioned earlier. Meeting adjourned."

With that, Councillor Pinkerton and the others made their way back behind their private closed door, leaving the people of Serenity to ease off their numb backsides, stretch their arms and talk excitedly amongst themselves.

Hugo stepped in and took Amber's elbow. Gently. Respectfully. But that didn't stop the sparks of heat from travelling up her arm and making a mess of her synapses as he tilted his head to murmur near her ear.

"You can't possibly believe I want Serenity to suffer."

"You have no idea what I believe. You don't know me at all."

His eyes didn't move but she imagined them sliding up and down her body as a slow smile tugged at the corners of his mouth. "You have a short memory, Ms Hartley. Or perhaps selective would be a better description."

"You want words? I can think of so many words to describe you right now, *Your Highness*. We could go on like this *all night long*."

Hugo's eyes darkened. And yep, she'd heard it too. Dragon fire gathered behind Amber's teeth as conflict and desire swirled through her like a maelstrom. But behind it all, the need to protect her town, her people, herself.

"Game on," said Hugo as he was swallowed by the crowd.

Bring it on, Amber thought as she crossed her arms and backed away. Bring. It. On.

CHAPTER THREE

HUGO TUGGED HIS cap lower over his eyes and hunched into his shoulders as he made his way up a gravel path winding through the quaint market town of Serenity. The kind of place where business hours varied daily and where as many animals sat behind counters as people.

Prospero—the bodyguard Hugo's uncle had insisted upon—was not happy about it. He did not like being in the open. Or moving slowly. Or places with tall buildings. Or cars with open windows. He particularly didn't like the fact that Hugo had ditched him in Vallemont a couple of months before and had only just made contact again, requesting his presence, now that he had been outed.

But for all the big guy's efforts at keeping Hugo safe, Hugo blamed him for the sideways glances and double-takes. The size of a telephone box, dressed in head-to-toe black, a clean-shaven head and *Men in Black* sunglasses, he looked like a soccer hooligan on steroids.

Otherwise there was no way the locals would make the connection between the guy in the ripped jeans, Yankees cap and skateboard shoes and the Prince in the three-piece suit from the meeting the night before.

Though it wouldn't take long for that to change. There was no doubt the story of Hugo's public life was being shared and spread.

A prince, fifth in line to the throne of the principality of Vallemont. An Australian mother, a father who had died when his son was fifteen, having infamously run his car off a cliff with his young mistress at the wheel. Now he was the black sheep: independently wealthy and single.

The official palace statement was that Hugo was back at work, but after the wedding debacle he'd needed to escape. Eventually he'd found himself in Serenity. Where his mother had been born.

Days had dissolved into nights, a blur of time and quiet and nothingness; of exploring the empty, echoing house which seemed uninspired by his presence as if he too were a ghost.

Until he'd walked over the other side of the hill and found a hammock strung between two trees in the shade. He'd sat down, kicked off his shoes and fallen asleep.

Upon waking, he'd looked into a pair of whisky-brown eyes. And seen colour for the first time in as long as he could rightly remember.

"Alessandro!"

Hugo followed his name to find Councillor Pinkerton sitting at a colourful wrought-iron table inside a place calling itself "Tansy's Tea Room", which looked like a middle-eastern opium den.

She waved him in and, since he needed her support to be granted planning permission for his resort, he entered, leaving Prospero at the door with a, "Stay. Good boy."

"Sit," said the councillor. "Have some tea. You look tired. A man as rich and good-looking as you should never look tired. It gives the rest of us nothing to aspire to." She clicked her fingers, called out, "A top-up on my 'Just Do It', and a 'Resurrection' for my friend, please."

"Should I be afraid?" he asked.

"It's just tea. Mostly chamomile. I'm on your side."

"Glad to hear it."

"Don't get me wrong, I'm on Ms Hartley's side too."

"I see."

"Do you?"

"You want what is best for Serenity."

"I do."

"Councillor?"

"Paulina, please."

"Paulina. Before the town meeting last night, your council had seemed extremely positive about my proposal."

"They were."

"And now? Is a green light still assured, or are we now leaning towards…khaki?"

The councillor smiled. "I can see that the resort would be good for us. An influx of tourists means an influx of the kind of money which cannot be sneezed at for a town of our size. But Ms Hartley had a point. The beauty of Serenity is its way of living. The openness, the quiet, the kindness and, most of all, the community. We are self-sufficient in the most important ways, in a great part thanks to the commune."

"I would have thought the presence of a commune has negative connotations in this day and age."

"Which is why we call it an 'Inclusive Community' on the brochures."

Two pots of tea landed on their table, slopping towards the rims as the unsteady table rocked.

Paulina poured. "So how is your mother?"

Hugo stilled at the unexpected turn of conversation. "My mother?"

"Anna. Yes. I knew her, you know. Before." She waggled her fingers as if about to go back in time. "We were good mates, in fact. Went through school together, met boys together. So how is she?"

Hugo went to say *Fine*, but something about this woman, her bluntness, the intelligence in her eyes, the fact she'd known Hugo's mother in the before, had him saying, "I think she's lonely."

"Hmm. She is remarried, no?"

"Yes."

"To a French businessman, I hear?"

"An importer, yes. He travels a great deal."

"Ah." The councillor nodded again. "Handsome though, I expect. Your father was a very handsome man. I might even go so far as to say, devastatingly so. Add the Giordano charm and..." Paulina pursed her lips and blew out a long, slow stream of air.

"So I have heard."

Paulina's eyes hardened. Then she slapped herself on the hand. "Sorry. Insensitive."

Hugo waved a hand, releasing her of any apology.

His father *had* been charming, famously so. His mother was only one of the women who'd loved him for it. The mistress who'd been driving the car that had killed him was another.

"I was there the day they met. Your mother and father. Would you care to hear the tale?"

Since Hinterland House, with its air of quiet slumber, had not yet given up any secrets, he found he cared a great deal.

"Your father was ostensibly in Australia to see the reef and the rock and forge relationships on behalf of his little-known country—but mostly to watch sports and try his fair share of our local beers. He came to our small corner to pick peaches. Your mother and I were working at the orchard that summer, handing out lemonade to the tourists. I remember so many long-limbed Germans, sweet-talking French, Americans full of bravado. And there was your father—the brooding Prince.

"A good girl, your mother. Seriously shy, she ignored his flirtation, which was a good part of why he kept it up. He could have offered diamonds, played up his natural charisma, but he was cleverer than that. He brought her hand-picked wild flowers, notes scratched into sheaves of paper bark, the very best peach he picked every day. It took three days. When she fell, she fell hard. And I was glad to see his adoration didn't diminish for having her. They were so very much in love.

"He left for Sydney a week later. A week after that he came back for her with a ring and a proposal. And I never saw her again."

Paulina smiled. "I was sorry to hear of his passing, not only for your mother's sake. How old were you?"

"Fifteen," Hugo said without having to think about it. His headmaster had been the one to inform him, having been instructed by his uncle to wait until after the funeral. A decision had been made not to send Hugo home to keep him away from the scandal.

"Ah. A trying period in the life of a boy, at the best of times."

Hugo merely nodded.

"Ah," said the councillor, looking over Hugo's shoulder, a smile creasing the edges of her eyes as someone approached their table.

Hugo knew who it was before a word was said. The wild energy snapping at the air behind him disturbed the hairs on the back of his neck.

He let his voice travel as he said, "Now, Paulina, about that woman who stood up in front of the council last night—shall I buy the bag of lime and shovel or simply pay you back?"

The councillor's eyes widened in surprise before a smile creased her face. "Good morning, Ms Hartley."

A beat, then, "Good morning, Councillor Pinkerton."

"Paulina, please."

Hugo pressed back his chair and stood. Amber wore a short summer dress that hung from her tanned shoulders by thin ribbons tied at her shoulders. A battered pork-pie hat sat atop her head, leaving her long honey-blonde hair to hang in waves over one shoulder.

But it was the eyes that got him every time. They were devastating. Fierce, wanton bedroom eyes that could lay civilisations to waste.

"Well, if it isn't my worthy adversary," he said.

Amber tilted her chin and looked only at Hugo's companion. "I'm so glad to have run into you, Paulina. I was hoping to have a word."

"Any time. Won't you join us?"

Amber's chin lifted. "Considering the subject, I don't think that's wise."

"I think quite the opposite. Did the two of you manage to meet properly last night?"

Hugo looked to Amber with a smile, allowing her to respond.

She gaped like a fish out of water before saying, slowly, "We did not meet last night."

"Then allow me. Amber, this is Prince Alessandro Giordano of Vallemont. Prince Alessandro, this is our supplier of all things sweet and honeyed, Amber Hartley."

"A pleasure to meet you." Hugo held out a hand. Amber's face was a concerto of emotion as she fought against the need to play nice, at least in front of others, so she didn't look like an ass.

Finally, Amber's eyes turned his way. "Prince *Alessandro*, was it?"

He nodded. "My friends call me Hugo."

"How nice for them." Then she took his hand, grabbed a hunk of skirt and curtseyed. Deeply. "Your Highness."

Until that moment Hugo hadn't realised a curtsey could be ironic. Laughter knocked against his windpipe, desperate to escape. Only years of maintaining a neutral countenance in affairs of state made it possible to swallow it down.

"Amber, sit," said Paulina. "I insist. Talk to the

man. Work out your grievances. At least attempt to come up with a workable plan, for your sake and for the sake of the town. If you can't, well, you can tick 'having tea with a prince' off your bucket list."

Councillor Pinkerton pushed back her chair and stood. Hugo reached for his wallet.

"No," said the older woman. "My treat. Wouldn't want anyone thinking you'd bribed me with a pot of tea, now, would we?"

Then she held out her hand, offering the seat to Amber.

"No," said Amber, waving both hands to make it clear she meant it. "Thank you. But I couldn't."

"Your loss," said the councillor. Then, at the door she called, "She's got mettle, this one. Might take more than a peach."

Hugo's laugh left his throat before he even felt it coming. Then he ran a hand up the back of his neck, settling the hairs that were still on edge.

Amber continued to glare.

"Please join me. At the very least so that I don't have to stand here all day."

"You'd like that, wouldn't you, *Prince Alessandro*? Get some paparazzi shots of us hanging together so as to muddy the waters regarding my side of the case."

"It's Hugo. Paparazzi a fixture here in downtown Serenity?"

"Well, no. But now word is out that you are here I'm sure it won't be long."

Hugo was sure of it too, meaning his blissful few weeks of anonymity truly were over. And the time to get the plans put to bed was ticking down.

"I'm going to sit," he said. "The chair is yours if you want it."

Amber glanced around, found the table beside his was empty, and sat there instead. With her back to him.

She turned her head ever so slightly. "This isn't the first time for you, is it?"

"Hmm? I didn't catch that with you sitting all the way over there." First time for what? he wondered. Drinking tea that smelled like feet? Or locking horns with a stubborn woman he couldn't get out of his head? "First time for what?"

"Tearing the heart and soul out of a town and turning it into some fancy, homogenised getaway for the idle rich."

"Ah. I probably won't use that as the tagline of any future advertising, but yes, I have experience in this area. This will be my…seventh such resort." A beat, then, "Have you been Googling me, Amber?"

Her shoulders rolled. "It was a stab in the dark. The only semi-decent Wi-Fi around here is at Herb's Shiatsu Parlour. You can go grey waiting for a picture to load."

"But at least you'd feel relaxed while doing so."

Her mouth twitched before she turned her back on him again. He spotted the edge of the dandelion tattoo that curled delicately over her shoulder blade. He remembered the slight rise of it as he'd run a thumb over the area once. The way her muscles reacted, contracting under his touch.

"I've come up against people like you before," she said, "privileged, successful, glowing with an aura that says *don't worry, I've done this before, you're in good hands*. But just because you think you're in the right, doesn't mean that you are."

"I could say the same for you."

"I live in a shack, Your Highness. I collect and sell honey for a living. You and are I are not on the same playing field. But the biggest difference is that, while you think you are in the right, I know I am."

Hugo could have argued relativism till the cows came home. In fact, if they'd been rugged up in her bed, limbs curled around one another, it might even have been fun.

"What were you telling Councillor Pinkerton about me?" Amber asked, and Hugo gave up pretending he could focus on anything else while she was near.

He pushed his tea aside and turned back to face her. "Until the moment you arrived your name did not come up."

"I find that hard to believe."

"Are you a subject of much chatter around these parts?"

A pause. "No. Maybe. At one time. I was a newcomer too once."

"The councillor and I weren't talking about my plans at all. It turns out she knew my mother. And my father."

Talk of family? Talk of something personal? He half expected Amber to leap over the table and bolt. But her head turned a little further, giving Hugo a view of her profile. Full lips, neat nose, and a fine jaw disappearing into swathes of golden hair. When she lowered her eyes he was hit with the memory of her sleeping; hands curled under her ear, lips softly parted, lashes creating smudges of shadow against her cheeks.

She asked, "Was that a surprise?"

"It was. A good one, though."

She turned a fraction more on her chair, until her eyes found his. Big, brazen pools of whisky that he knew, from experience, darkened with desire and brightened when she laughed. "Prince Alessandro—"

"Don't do that." Hugo's voice dropped so that only she could hear. "Amber, I am still the same man you found sleeping in your hammock and took into your home. Into your bed. I am still Hugo."

Amber's throat worked as she swallowed. "Ah. But that's the name your friends call you. And I am not your friend."

"You could be." Hugo called upon years of royal conditioning to keep his messier emotions at bay, to keep himself apart. He leant towards her, close enough to see the creases now furrowing her brow, the single freckle on her neck, the way her lashes tangled as they curled. "I'd like it very much if you were."

Her chest rose and fell as her eyes darted between his. She licked her lips then glanced away. "You have history here, I understand that. But you're not the only one. Think on that as you sit in your big house, poring over your Machiavellian scheme to destroy this community."

"You paint quite the picture. You must have spent a great deal of time imagining what I've been up to since you threw me out."

Pink raced up her cheeks as her jaw clenched. "I can assure you, *Prince Alessandro*, the amount of time I have spent wondering about you is entirely proportional to my desire to figure out how to make you walk away for good."

"Hmm," he said, not believing it for a second. The deep breaths, the darkness in her eyes—she was still as aware of him as he was of her. As much as she might want to switch off the fascination they had in one another, it was still alive and well.

"Amber?"

Amber blinked several times before they both turned towards a man with raging red hair gelled into painful-looking spikes. "Tansy. Hi. Sorry, I'm taking up a table. I…"

Amber stopped when she realised that was clearly not Tansy's concern. For Tansy was staring at Hugo as if he were an alien who'd landed a spaceship inside his shop. And behind him Tansy had amassed a small crowd, a veritable sea of tie-dye and hemp.

"Is this…?" said Tansy. "Is he…?"

"Why, yes," said Amber, her voice nice and loud. "Tansy, this is Prince Alessandro Giordano, the man who is planning on stripping our hill bare."

Tansy shoved a hand between them. "So pleased to meet you, Your Highness."

"Hugo, please. My friends call me Hugo."

When the shake was done, Tansy's heavily tattooed hands fluttered to his heart. "A prince. In my tea room. I honestly don't know what to say."

"How about *Get out*?" said Amber as she hopped out of the seat and melted into the crowd. "How about *Leave our village be*? How about *We don't want your type here*?"

Hugo saw Prospero begin to head inside, clearly

not liking the growing crowd. Hugo stayed him with a shake of the head.

"Will you be King?" asked a woman twirling her hair and looking at him as if he were a hot lunch.

Hugo searched the crowd until he saw Amber's profile. She was whispering to someone in the back, no doubt working them to her favour.

"No," said Hugo. "Vallemont is a principality, not a kingdom. It is protected and overseen by a royal family, the head of which is my uncle, the Sovereign Prince. There are several people between me and the crown."

A ripple of disappointment swept through the small crowd.

Hugo bit back a laugh. He heard that. But since his chance at a possible shot at the crown had been ripped away from him at the age of fifteen, he'd had to find other uses for himself. Building resorts gave his life meaning.

"Now, who here loves a lagoon? Tennis courts? Who thinks this town could do with a yoga studio?"

He no longer kept looking for Amber, but he could feel her glaring at him just fine.

Dying sunlight poured tracks of gold over the stone floor of the tiny little shopfront in Serenity she had inherited along with the beehives when she'd first arrived in town.

Honey-Honey was a teeny-tiny mud hut with a desk, an old-fashioned cash register that binged winningly as it opened, and a small back room behind a curtain. The shop floor boasted a handful of shelves filled to the brim with pots of honey and beeswaxy goodness. And Ned, who was curled up on his soft doggy bed in the sunniest corner, his face twitching as he dreamed of chasing dandelion fluff and finding an endless supply of used socks.

Amber's ancient broom tossed dust motes into the light as she swept the stone floor, preparing to close up shop for the day, when she looked up and saw a man in black as big as a house, the man she'd seen hovering around Hugo at the town meeting and again at Tansy's.

"Amber."

So busy gaping, Amber hadn't seen Hugo lurking behind him until it was too late.

Ned on the other hand was all over him— bouncing about on his back feet, nose nuzzling Hugo's hand, tail wagging as if he was in utter bliss. The big man with Hugo looked ready to take down the dog at the first sign of teeth.

"Ned, heel." She clicked her fingers, knowing he'd feel the vibration if he didn't hear her words, and Ned gave her a side eye before ambling to her feet and plopping to his haunches with a snort. His version of a doggy eye-roll. "We're closed."

"This is the honey we collected?"

She winced at the use of "we". "Some. Several local apiaries sell their wares in this space. Different bees, different flora, make for different tastes, different texture, different healing properties." Amber tugged the strap of her bag over her head until it angled across her body. Not as if it was some kind of shield. Righteousness was all the armour she needed. "What are you doing here? I said all I needed to say at the tea room."

"I didn't. Are those live bees in the wall?"

He peered through the dark hexagonal observation pane where a small hive of bees buzzed and worked. Huffing out a breath, Amber turned on the nearest lamp, creating a pool of gold on the floor and showcasing the sweet little hive in her wall.

Hugo pressed a finger towards the glass but didn't touch. The one person she'd ever seen think before leaving a fingerprint she'd have to clean.

Humming contentedly, he moved around the space, picking up tubs of wax, reading over the names of the several flavours of honey. "Amber, this is charming. Why didn't you tell me about this place when we were…?" Hugo waved a hand to intimate the rest.

"Hooking up?" she finished helpfully.

The man in black squeaked, then covered it with a manly cough.

Hugo turned, ignoring his big friend, his eyes only for Amber. "Is that what we were doing?"

"Sure. Why? What else would you call it?"

Amber tucked her hair behind her ear and feigned nonchalance, even while her knees started to tingle at the way he was looking at her. But he didn't offer an alternative. He did rub at his hand, no doubt aching from having shaken the hand of every person in town since his "disguise" had been blown. Traitors. Fawning over the enemy just because of an accident of birth. And charm. And those magnetic good looks.

She pressed her palm to her belly and rolled her shoulders.

The townsfolk might all be blinded by the trappings but not her. She could take him down all on her own. They'd thank her for it later.

He rubbed at his hand again, wincing this time.

"Oh, for Pete's sake." Amber turned on her heel and went to the freezer behind the curtain in the back, grabbed a bucket and filled it with ice. She plonked the bucket onto her counter and clicked her fingers at Hugo.

He came as asked.

"Good boy."

A solitary eyebrow shot north. Amber tried her dandiest to remember that she didn't find the move seriously sexy. Not any more.

When Amber looked back at Hugo it was to

find his gaze had dropped to her smile, where it stayed for a beat or two. Her lips tingled under the attention, remembering how that look usually ended. Heat trickled through her veins and she began to itch all over, her body wanting what it could no longer have.

"Give me your hand," she demanded, all business.

He looked at his hand, surprised to find he'd been rubbing it. Then he looked at the bucket of ice. "I don't think so."

"Don't be such a baby."

The big guy made another strangled noise in the doorway, though this one sounded more like a laugh.

"Have you never had this done before?"

"I'm usually better protected."

The laughter from the doorway came to an abrupt halt.

Amber took her chance, grabbed Hugo's hand, and before the warmth of his skin, the familiarity of his touch, overcame her she shoved it into the ice.

Hugo let forth a string of expletives, in multiple languages no less. Amber enjoyed every one. Hugo shifted from foot to foot and cleared his throat.

"You okay there, buddy?"

"Peachy," he muttered.

And she shoved his hand just a little deeper. "So who's the elephant in the room?"

"Hmm?"

"The giant who is trying very, very hard not to tackle me right now."

"That would be Prospero. My bodyguard."

"Why the heck do you need a bodyguard?"

Hugo raised the single eyebrow.

She raised one right back. "Seriously. If you were a president or a drug lord or something, sure. Are you afraid the townspeople will throw mantras at you? Or is this because of *me*? Wow. Does he have a dossier on me? What's my code name?"

Hugo's brow furrowed, reminding her of the Furrows of Important Dreams on the day they had first met. That gravity that had drawn her to him in the first place. It was almost enough for her to let it go. Almost.

"Why do you need a bodyguard? I really want to know."

"Last year my uncle and his family were having a picnic by a local waterfall when a band of masked men attacked. Whether to kidnap, scare or worse, it was never clear. The small security detail managed to fend them off but the perpetrators got away. The royal family upped security across the board. Prospero has been my devoted body man ever since. Though I believe he feels as if he must have done something terrible in a former life to end up on my detail. Right, big guy?"

Aw, crud. "Was anyone hurt?"

"Not physically, no. But my uncle has been hyper-vigilant ever since, making demands on the family no one in power should ever make."

Amber had a thought. "Is he the one making you turn Serenity into a resort?"

Hugo smiled. "No. In fact, when he finds out he will not be pleased."

"Why?"

"Because every decision he makes is for the good of Vallemont. This decision is for the good of me."

"No kidding."

It was hard to get her head around. For Amber had known him before he was royal. Or at least before she'd *known* he was royal. The point was she'd known him when he was *Hugo*. A man of unremitting curiosity, acerbic wit and nothing but time. An avid listener with an easy smile. Smart as anyone she'd ever met, including her parents, who were called on to untangle the trickiest international laws on a daily basis. But, basically, a dissolute gadabout.

Yet he was a successful businessman in his own right. He accepted a bodyguard because he was deemed important to the crown and yet was content to stand up to his uncle if he believed it was the right thing to do.

While her brain understood the duality, a small part of her was still clinging on to the man who'd cleaned out her gutters when he'd seen grey clouds on the horizon; who'd rubbed her feet without being asked as they'd snuggled on her ancient couch.

She'd kicked that man out of her bed.

And created an adversary.

No. He'd done that. He wanted to build this resort of his for his own ends. She was merely standing up for what she believed was right.

Hugo made to lift his hand from the ice and she grabbed it. "Stop moving." She wasn't done with him just yet. "So this bodyguard of yours. Where was he when we were...?"

She flapped a hand.

"I was playing hooky."

"From?"

"Real life."

"Seriously?"

"You keep questioning the veracity of my answers. I have no reason to lie to you, Amber. I never have. All you ever had to do was ask."

She shook her head, but didn't have a comeback. It wasn't the first time she'd been accused of avoiding intimacy, but it was the first time she stuck around to continue talking to the person who'd made the accusation.

She told herself it was a learning opportunity. How not to get fooled next time. Next time what? Next time she found a hot man in her hammock and dragged him back to her cave to have her way with him for a few weeks?

Cheeks heating, she gritted her teeth. "From the little I know of Vallemont, it sounds like one of the prettiest spots in Europe. All craggy mountains and verdant valleys? Am I right?"

Hugo nodded.

"So, as far as real life goes, being a prince of such a realm must have been terrible. And being rich and handsome and royal surely feels all the same after a while."

His smile turned to laughter—rough and soft, so that she felt it right deep down inside.

"Alas, now real life has found you again," she said, "you have to go back to princeing. Is that the right verb?"

"You done?"

"For now."

"Good. Because it's my turn. Are you ready to tell me how you ended up here yet?"

Amber flinched. And said nothing.

"Nothing? Really? I showed you mine, now you show me yours. Quid pro quo. Or else I'm no longer the bad guy for not sharing my life story."

Dammit. He had her there.

"So what were you running away from?"

"Who said I was running away?"

"Those of us who are not where we started are all running from something. Responsibility. Danger. Boredom. So which was it?"

"I didn't run," she said, the words feeling as though they were being pulled from her throat with pliers. "I had an honest-to-goodness chance at a fresh start so I took it. I wasn't running, I was exploring."

"To what end?"

"It didn't even matter. It was all new for me out there. And all mine."

She knew she wasn't making sense to anyone but herself, but Hugo didn't press. He had a way of knowing just how far to push before giving her breathing space. She'd never met anyone who could read her the way he did.

Feeling as if a spotlight was shining on her, about to give her deepest insecurities and darkest fears away, she glanced over Hugo's shoulder to the shadow in the doorway. "So how did he summon you, Prospero? Did he send up a bat signal? Or would that be a crown signal? One in the shape of a ceremonial sword, perhaps?"

"He used a telephone signal, ma'am."

"How modern. I hadn't realised he even had a phone. Or a title, for that matter."

Hugo laughed deep in his throat, only just loud enough for her to catch it. The way it was when they'd lain in bed at night. The way it was when he'd swept her hair from the back of her neck to find that kiss spot that brought her out in goosebumps, before murmuring all the things he planned to do to her the next moment he could get her naked.

In the quiet that followed, Amber held her breath, hoping Hugo had no clue where her thoughts had gone. His charm was dangerous. His likeability her liability. His power, his political and personal influence, a real, living thing.

People like Hugo, like her own parents, were used to getting their way.

Not this time.

Not on her watch.

"And what exactly did our friend *the Prince* tell you about where he had been, Prospero? And what he had been up to?"

Prospero shot a slightly panicked look to his boss. "His Highness does not kiss and tell."

Amber burst out laughing. "Meaning he did exactly that. I never mentioned kisses, and nobody else in town knew about any kisses, so that leaves him." Amber waggled a hand Hugo's way.

Hugo caught her gaze, held it. "You really didn't tell anyone about what had kept you so busy the last few weeks? Not a girlfriend? A sha-man? A friendly possum?"

Amber folded her arms loosely across her chest and slowly shook her head.

"More's the pity. My reputation could do with some bolstering in this town."

She laughed again. "Not going to happen."

"Really? You haven't been fighting the desperate urge to drop into casual conversation that I am a man of experience."

"No."

"And taste." His gaze dropped to her mouth before lifting back to her eyes. His expression darkening, all touches of humour now gone. "And unparalleled skill?"

"Hugo."

He paused. A slow, warm smile spreading across his face and making her knees shiver. Because—dammit!—she'd called him Hugo. She'd been so determined to stick with *Your Highness*.

"Amber," he lobbied, with grave deliberation.

His deep voice, the crinkle around his eyes, did things to her basic structure. Turning her bones to liquid. Quieting her worries. Until she felt as if she was floating just a little above the ground.

She cleared her throat. "How's your hand?"

"Numb."

Rolling her eyes, Amber dragged his hand from

the ice, feeling a little bit better when he winced. "And now?"

Hugo wriggled his fingers, twisted his hand and grinned at her.

She grabbed a tea towel and threw it at him. "Try not to drip. I've just swept. Now, while this has been a delight, you really must leave. It's time Ned and I got home."

Hugo wiped his hand. And nodded. "Fine. But first, the reason I came by. I brought you this." He held out his hand and Prospero handed over a rolled-up sheaf of papers held together with a pink and gold ribbon.

Amber looked at it warily. "What is it?"

"Take it home. Look it over. We can talk about it tomorrow. Once you've had time to think."

"I've thought. I don't want to talk to you tomorrow. Unless it's to hear you say you were mistaken and you're sorry for causing our quiet little community such distress. And that you are leaving and never coming back."

Hugo's eyes darkened. And he took a step closer. Or maybe he didn't. Maybe he just looked at her in that intense, indulgent way she found so overwhelming. As if she'd been tumbled by a rogue wave, not sure if she'd find her feet ever again.

"Fine," she said, whipping out a hand to take the sheaf of paper. Taking care not to let her fingers touch his. Those fingers had a way of stripping her defences and right now those defences were all she had.

When Hugo stepped back she felt that too. As though someone had pulled a blanket from her shoulders, and a stone from her chest.

He turned to leave before looking back. "Amber."

Swallowing his name, she simply waited.

"Is fighting this what the town needs? Is it even what they want?"

Amber reeled. "Of course it is."

"They seemed pretty happy about the idea at the meeting."

"They were happy a real live prince was in their midst. And you knew they would be. Why else did you shave? And wear that slick suit? And give them your smile?"

"My smile?"

"You know the one. All teeth and charm and eye crinkles. You are well aware that it makes knees go wobbly from a thousand paces."

Amber found herself glad the light was low, otherwise the look in his eyes might have melted her on the spot.

"I know perfectly well how stubborn you are, Amber. And how much you care. Take care you don't lose yourself inside a blind crusade."

Amber flinched. Hugo could not have picked better words with which to cut her. Deep. The number of times she'd accused her parents of getting caught up in doing right, in fighting for the little people, in pursuing justice at all costs, without really stopping to imagine the consequences...

She stamped her foot so that Ned would come to her side and lost her hand in the familiar softness of his fur. "I know what I'm doing."

"Okay, then." He reached a hand to the doorjamb, breathed, and turned back to her one last time. "You were quite the sight up there at the town meeting. Banging on the lectern. Riling the masses. I was waiting for you to climb the thing and punch your hand in the air. If you had I am absolutely certain the council would have agreed to anything. Including running me out of town with flaming pitchforks."

Amber breathed. Or at least she tried. Her throat threatened to close down. She wasn't good at taking compliments, never having had reason to learn when she was a kid.

With that he tapped his knuckles on the counter, gave Prospero a look and left.

Leaving Amber all alone with her weak knees, her deaf dog and the insatiable hunger that was gnawing at her insides.

Though it wasn't for food. Not even a bit.

CHAPTER FOUR

"IS THAT A HELIPAD?" Johnno's voice hummed at the corner of Amber's brain as she sat back in one of Sunflower's straw-filled beanbags and rubbed at her temples, breathing in the scent of Sunflower's stew warming over the brazier near her feet.

"And stables. Look!" That was Sunflower, resident animal whisperer, her fey voice tinged with excitement.

But Amber didn't want to look. She wanted to figure out what it meant that Hugo had given her the architectural plans in the first place. Plans so detailed they had clearly been worked on for some time.

"Does he think I'll go all gooey at the fact he has given away a big chunk of advantage? Does he think I'm that easy?"

"Honey," said Sunflower. "Who are you talking about?"

She flung her arm away from her eyes and said, "Hugo!"

At the concerned faces of her friends, her comrades, these sweet, trusting souls, she remembered everyone else knew him as Prince Alessandro Giordano of Vallemont. "The Prince. The Prince gave them to me."

"Oh, my."

Amber sat forward as best she could in the lumpy homemade beanbag. Firelight sent long, scary shadows over Sunflower's brightly painted caravan beyond. "You all agree, right? That we need to fight this? I'm not on some kind of blind crusade."

"Oh, yes." Sunflower swayed side to side to the music in her head.

"Johnno?"

"Hmm? Sure thing. I only wish he was dastardly. It'd be easier to dislike the guy."

Sunflower leaned down to give her man a hug. Then shoved a bowl of stew under Amber's nose. "You look pale. Eat."

Knowing better than to argue, Amber ate, spooning mouthfuls of unexpected vegetables and some kind of gamey meat into her mouth.

While Sunflower said, "Everyone does seem to be stuck on how charming he is. And how handsome. Do you think he's handsome?"

Johnno nodded.

Amber loved these people with every recess of her stone-cold heart, but at times she wished they were a bit more commercially switched on.

"Don't you think he's handsome, Amber?" Sunflower asked.

She put the half-eaten stew on the ground. "Sure. I guess." *Handsome didn't even come close.* "But what that has to do with any of this, I have no idea."

"Don't you?"

Something in Sunflower's voice made Amber wonder exactly how much she had been paying attention. Was it possible she'd known Hugo was in Amber's bed the morning she'd come by? That Ned hadn't been the one making the banging noises?

If any of them knew she'd been the one feeding him and watering him while he made his devious plans she was sure they'd never look at her the same way again.

Then Sunflower grabbed a set of bowls to hold the corners of the plans down. "I just don't see it. Far too clean-cut for my taste. Not like my darling scruffy Johnno. Though it is hard to believe he was left at the altar."

"He was what, now?" said Amber.

"Left at the altar by a runaway bride."

Amber looked from one friend to the next to find them nodding along. "How did you even know about this?"

Johnno stuck a stick in the fire and sparks shot up into the sky. "Everyone knows."

Amber let out a breathy, "Jeez…"

Playing hooky from real life, my ass.

"So this was recent?"

"Oh, yes."

When he'd opened his eyes and looked into hers that very first day, she'd had to brace herself so as not to fall right into his gaze. For she'd felt his pain in that unguarded moment as if it had been her own.

Like a standing redwood suffering the notches of an axe. Not broken so much as wounded. Needing somewhere safe to hole up. To heal. It had been half the reason she'd thrown caution to the wind and invited him into her home.

Had she been a transition fling? Why the heck did it matter?

Because you're envious of some other woman who turfed him out, when you should be high-fiving her. Starting an exclusive club—women who've turned away the estimable right-royal Hugo.

Sunflower went on, oblivious, "As the story went, he handled it like a true gentleman, not saying a bad word about the girl. A few days later they did a television interview together. It was honest, forgiving. Turns out they're old friends and they both wished the very best to one another for the future."

Sadie. The fact that this mystery woman had a name felt like a dagger to Amber's stomach. Which was ridiculous. Amber had no hold over Hugo. And he none over her. Her stomach would simply have to catch up.

"He might be the big bad wolf, but boy, does he make it look appealing."

Amber dropped her head into her hands and let out a sorry sob.

"Hey," said Johnno, back with them. "Doesn't this design remind you of a honeycomb shape?"

Of course she had noticed.

"Oh, my," Sunflower breathed, glancing at Amber. "How about that?"

"And did you also see where the buildings are situated? Right here, on this exact spot." The colourful caravans, shanties, tents, tree houses and demountables obliterated by the stroke of a pen. As if they'd never been.

Just about the only section of the hill which had been preserved were the two trees to which her hammock was hitched.

Rubbing the heels of her palms deep into her eyes, she tried to hold back the memory, but it came anyway.

It had been late afternoon. The air had been filled with pollen and that strange heaviness that heralded a storm.

She'd snapped off a chunk of honeycomb and given it to him. He'd carried it back through the forest to the shack, holding it up to the sun, rubbing it between his fingers, licking the thing till she'd tripped over her own feet.

Somehow they'd ended up at the hammock.

then in the hammock. Together. It had been one of the most perfect moments of her entire life.

And then it hit her. *That* was why he'd given her the plans.

He knew she'd see that he'd saved those trees. *That manipulative bastard.*

She was furious she hadn't seen it straight away. She'd been raised by master manipulators after all.

Her parents, Bruce and Candace Grantley—OBEs—had been "influencers" before the term was popular. On the surface that seemed like a compliment. A sign of respect. But really it meant they knew how to sway, cajole, manoeuvre, distract, use bias to engineer outcomes to their liking.

Embroiled in an international child labour case, they'd begun bringing Amber along to newspaper photo shoots, on television interviews, using her as an example of a child of privilege. A counterpoint to the children they were representing in some far-off country. But only after taking her braces off five months early. She'd overheard her mother telling her father a bright white smile would "play better".

Now, at twenty-seven, she had bottom teeth that overlapped. Just a little. Just enough to remind her the lengths her parents had gone to in order to get their way.

"True gentleman my ass," Amber muttered,

sweeping the plans up into her arms, shoving them under her arm and taking off up the hill.

Hugo sat on the large portico at the rear of Hinterland House, watching the dragonflies dance over the surface of the moonlit fountain beyond.

His phone buzzed. A quick check showed him it was from his aunt Marguerite.

He ignored it.

He'd been getting messages from the palace—mostly from his aunt—since he'd first taken off. He'd made it clear he had no intention of telling them where he was until he was ready.

He was a grown man. And not near enough to the throne for his whereabouts to matter to anyone but his mother. He was in one piece, he was keeping his head down, and after recent events he needed some time. And he would very much appreciate it if they'd leave him the hell alone.

When the phone buzzed again, he switched it off.

Prospero came outside with a green metal coil and a box of matches. He lit the end until a whirl of sweet-smelling smoke curled into the air.

"What is that?" Hugo asked.

"They call it a mozzie coil. One of the women in town gave it to me earlier when she saw my bites." Prospero tugged a black sleeve up to his elbow, revealing a handful of red welts.

"Do you need those seen to?"

The big man shook his head. "Just mosquitos. Saliva takes out the itch."

"Did the woman in town help you with that too?"

Even in the growing darkness Hugo saw the red creeping up the big man's throat.

He'd been in town a few days now. It would be worth getting his take on the situation. "So, Prospero, you have been paying attention." One could only hope. "What do you think of my plans?"

Prospero did his soldier poster move, looking out into the middle distance. "I couldn't say, Your Highness."

"You couldn't or you won't?"

"Yes, sir."

Smarter than he looked. "And what do you think of my opposition?"

"Sir?"

"Need I be worried about Amber Hartley?"

Prospero stilled. "In what way? Do you think she is dangerous? Has she threatened you again?"

"I don't think she is about to jump out of the bushes and attack me, if that's what you're worried about."

Prospero's face worked before he came to a decision. "You joke. I understand that. But you must know, Your Highness, that the possibility of someone jumping out of the bushes and attacking you is why I am here."

Hugo winced. Right. Bad choice of words.

As he had intimated to Amber, not that long ago his uncle, aunt and their multiple sets of twins had been near-victims of a targeted attack while on a family picnic within the palace grounds.

Hugo sat forward. "I am not blasé, Prospero. I promise. I have every intention of living a long and healthy life. If you feel that I am placed in any real danger, I will heed your concerns. Now, please tell me you understand I was joking. That Amber is not a physical threat."

A muscle twitched under Prospero's eye. "My observations suggest you do not see straight when it comes to Ms Hartley. You are not careful when you are with her."

Hugo blinked. "I believe you are right."

For Amber Hartley had been a safe haven when his life was in upheaval. A slip from reality when reality chased hot on his heels. No expectations, no burden, no demands. He could not have been more grateful that he had met her when he had. And that kind of thing left a mark.

Which didn't even begin to cover the way his blood still heated at the sight of her. How precisely he could remember the scent of her hair. The taste of her skin. How deeply satisfied he felt when he made her smile. Even fighting with her was the most fun he remembered having in years. *Years*

Yes, Amber Hartley had left a mark on him. A brand.

But he would not change his mind about the resort because of it. No matter how much he wished he'd had one more week in her bed.

While his father had been Sovereign Prince, Hugo had been the next successor. But when his father died he'd been too young to take the throne and his uncle had acceded instead, shunting him to sixth in line as his uncle's children now took precedence. It had forced Hugo to reimagine his life. It had taken time. He'd been angry for a while, had acted up, thrown money around. Until one of his wild investments had paid off. And just like that he'd found purpose. His resorts had seen stupendous success, channelling millions into the Vallemont economy and projecting the small, quiet principality into the international consciousness.

Families in Vallemont had safer jobs and better incomes, in thriving townships because of him. It was no crown, but it was a fine legacy, something of which he was immensely proud.

One he planned to keep refining, perfecting, until he made a true name for himself, by himself. Until the loss of the crown no longer mattered at all.

"Fear not the beautiful blonde in our midst, my intrepid friend. Once the resort plans are through council, my work here will be done and the project team will take over from there. We will head home."

Prospero wasn't the sharpest tool in the shed. Slipping away from him in Vallemont had been far too easy. But, as Hugo was beginning to find, he was a genuinely nice fellow.

"Do you feel as if you are being punished for something, having ended up with me, Prospero?"

Prospero swallowed and said, "I won't leave you. Not again."

"No. Of course. I totally understand. I just thought it would be a good opportunity to case the place. Perhaps see if any…women have an insight into the seedy underbelly of the town once the sun goes down."

Prospero looked to the door, then to Hugo, then to the door. "You keep your phone near by and you answer if I call."

"Yes, sir!"

"I see how you ignore the phone when the palace calls. Promise me."

Right. "Promise. Cross my heart. Hope to die."

His face looked pained at the thought. Big guy needed to lighten up.

"Lock all the doors. I will be back in an hour."

"Why don't you make it two?"

Hugo sat and listened to the rustle of wind in the trees, breathed in the sweet scent of gum trees and red dirt and wondered how he'd gone thirty-some years without feeding the Australian half of his soul.

The patter of feet on stone caught Hugo's attention moments before Ned bounded up onto the patio.

"Hey, Ned," Hugo said, leaning forward and opening his arms to the dog who came in for a cuddle.

Meaning his owner wouldn't be far behind.

Like a ghost she emerged from the shadows, skin glowing in the moonlight, hair floating behind her. A sylph, ethereal, so beautiful, Hugo's heart stuttered.

"Down, boy," Hugo murmured, pulling himself to standing.

While Ned, lovely, near-deaf Ned, who could pick up on human emotion from a mile away, dropped to his haunches in response.

"Okay," Hugo said, releasing him, after which the dog happily trotted off inside the house, then, "Well, if it isn't Amber Hartley, local beekeeper, representative of the little people, and excellent cooker of pancakes."

She baulked at the reference to the one time she'd cooked him breakfast before their cocoon had imploded. But then she collected herself and jogged up the back stairs and slammed a bunch of scrunched-up paper on the table beside him.

"Would that be the plans I gave to you earlier, rolled up all neat and tidy?"

"Sorry," she said, clearly not sorry at all. "I hope you have spares."

Hugo poked a thumb over his shoulder and Amber followed with her gaze. Her eyes widened when she saw the state-of-the-art computer system he'd set up on the Queen Anne dining table, the plans open right now on one of the three forty-inch monitors.

"I can't believe your gall!"

"Which gall?"

"Tennis courts. Seriously? And a spa? As for us, you levelled our part of the hill. As if we never existed."

"You didn't like it, then?"

"Like it? It made me feel physically ill!" She even looked a little grey, but it could have been the moonlight.

"And your friends? I'm assuming you shared the plans with them."

She snorted. "Johnno now wants his own helipad."

Interesting. "So what didn't *you* like about it? Be specific."

"Apart from the fact you plan to wipe out the commune in one fell swoop?"

"*Move* the commune."

"Excuse me?"

"There is a tract of land on the other side of town I had the planners put aside with space to build a number of cottages. More than enough to relocate everyone."

She blinked. "Those were meant for the commune? With the vegetable gardens? And neat little paths? The window sills filled with lavender?"

"Yes." Hugo realised he'd crossed his arms.

"Have you actually visited the hill? Apart from my place, of course."

The two of them locked eyes a moment, a spark zapping between them as they both remembered. Amber looked away first, tucking her hair behind her ear before frowning at the floor.

"Willow's caravan broke down on the hill twenty-five years ago. Tomas, her ex-husband, came down from Sydney to help her fix it and has lived in his tent next door ever since. Dozens of others have come and gone since. Sunflower and Johnno arrived a couple of years before I did. They'd been struggling to have kids for years, and coming here, to a place that was quiet and clean, helped them lick their wounds, to start afresh. Johnno lives in a tree house outside Sunflower's van. It could never be replicated. This community has been here long enough that nature has grown up around it. Grass and flowers and trees and shrubs connecting their homes to the earth. And you want to move them into matching cabins?"

"I'd be amenable to hearing input from the commune about the exact designs."

Amber ran a hand over her forehead, clearly not fine with it. And he knew that if he offered to move them an inch to the left but keep everything the same she'd still fight him.

"I don't have to make any concessions, Amber. The land is mine."

"I'm well aware—"

Hugo leaned forward. "I had my lawyers look into it. And by lawyers I mean the Sydney branch of the top firm in New York, so they are au fait with local law. Squatters' rights don't apply in your case."

She took so much time to speak he wondered how long she could hold her breath. "Why not?"

"I'm more than happy to give you a copy of their findings. It goes for over a hundred pages."

She held out a hand.

He coughed out a laugh. "I don't have one on me, but I promise I will get it to you."

Hugo pictured the plans for the estate. The vineyard that would sit so prettily on his side of the hill, the beautifully crafted structures taking advantage of the views on her side. The way his family's land, his mother's land, could be of use…h mother who had not felt much at all since his ther's death, merely going through the motio living her life. The way he could create some beautiful, functional, recreational and successful on his own. For her. And for himself. Without palace backing, palace oversight, or palace fingers delving into his financial pockets. He needed to do this. To create a legacy that was his alone.

With a growl, Amber plopped down in the cane chair beside his; legs stretched out in front of her, one arm bent behind her head, the other lying gently across her belly.

"That's it? You've given up? If I'd known it would be that easy I'd have got my lawyers onto you sooner."

"I come from a long line of lawyers; they do not scare me." She smiled from beneath the mask of her arm. "I'm just suddenly feeling very, very tired. Can we call a truce? For five minutes."

"Let's make it ten."

She held out her hand and he shook it. Holding on longer than necessary. Then again, she didn't let go either.

Finally, their hands parted, fingers sliding past one another, leaving tingles in their wake. And her hand once more moved to rest across her belly.

Watching her lie there, a picture of long-limbed, brown-skinned, earthy grace, he was well aware that there was something to be said for simply wanting *her*. She stirred and he dragged his hungry gaze away.

"Can you smell that?" she asked.

Hugo sniffed. "Cut grass? Night air?"

"Exactly. I don't know what it's like where you're from, but the cities I've lived in don't smell like this."

"No, they do not."

A pause, then, "What is it really like? Where you're from?"

"We have grass in Vallemont, like here. Night skies, like here."

"Fine...but—"

"Fine. It's...glorious! Tucked into a valley, surrounded by stunning mountains. Lakes like glass. Towns out of a Christmas card. With smart, sophisticated, friendly people. Last year we were also voted as having the cutest sheep on the planet."

"Sheep."

"Fluffy, white, say 'Baa' a lot."

The woman knew how to deadpan. "If it's so perfect over there, why did you really come here? And none of that 'playing hooky from real life' bull. Give me the unvarnished truth."

"So bolshie this evening." Her face was blank, but something—in her voice, in the shift of her body—alerted him. The town had been talking and she'd been listening. "You've visited Herb's Internet Café and Shiatsu Parlour, haven't you?"

She rolled her eyes. "I haven't Googled yo~ Why would I need to when you are right here

"Because you don't like asking hard quest~

when it might mean having to answer some of your own."

She growled again, this time shaking fists at the sky. "I thought princes were meant to be diplomatic."

"I thought hippies were meant to be mellow."

The growl turned to laughter. "You are infuriating, did you know that?"

"I've always thought myself rather charming."

"I'll bet." Her fists dropped, softening before her hands landed on her belly yet again. "The people in this place... For all its inherent loveliness, it's a small town. News travels fast and twists and turns as it goes. Whatever I might have heard, I'd prefer finding out the truth from the horse's mouth."

"Neigh."

She laughed again, then frowned at him as if she was struggling to figure him out. "Tell me about your wedding."

This time he had seen it coming. "You mean my non-wedding."

"If you like."

He sat forward, looked out into the dark night, and chose his words with care because this one wasn't all on him. "After the attack on my uncle he saw need to put his house in order, and so he offered me a deal. Marry or else."

"Or else what?"

"Being that she was born here, my mother is

not of royal blood. After my father died, her link to the royal household diminished. Once I turn thirty-three, it diminishes further. If I am not married by that date my place in the line of succession will be forfeited and my royal rights depreciated, making my mother's rights non-existent. With no prince as her husband, no prince as a son, her title would no longer have meaning. The palace—her home for the past thirty years—would no longer be available to her."

"You can't mean that he intended to kick her out?"

Hugo could feel Amber's sense of righteousness kick in. It flowed from her pores like the electricity that rumbled through the air around here right before a storm. He fed off it, releasing his own indignation, which he had kept held down deep inside all this time.

"Most unfair but there you have it."

"That's scandalous. It's…it's blackmail."

"Pretty much."

She shook her head; livid, riled, she could have been a Valkyrie. "I thought my parents were master manipulators, but your uncle takes the crown."

"Literally."

She looked to him then, a moment passing before she caught up. A smile passing over her bright eyes. "But you didn't marry."

"No, I did not."

"So, the girl. The woman. Your…" She flapped a hand at him, the way she did when she hit a thought she found too uncomfortable to voice. The fact that his ex-fiancée fell into that pile was interesting, to say the least.

"Sadie," Hugo said, "my intended, grew up in the palace, the daughter of a maid, and has been my best friend since as far back as I can remember. When I told her of my predicament she agreed to marry me out of the goodness of her heart, not for any romantic reason at all. But at the last she decided blackmail wasn't the best way to start a marriage. So she jumped out of a window at the palace and ran for the hills. On the way, a friend of mine—Will Darcy—found her on the side of the road, rescued her, whisked her away to safety, and the two of them fell madly in love."

"Oh. Wow. That news did *not* make it to Serenity."

"Small mercies."

"Were you—*are* you—okay with that?"

"Will and Sadie? I am immensely grateful they found one another. It let me off the hook big time."

He smiled, but she simply waited for him to stop joking and answer the question she'd asked.

"They are both wonderful people whom I care for very much. And I am truly happy for them both. Does that make me sound warm and generous, or a monster for not being broken-hearted?"

It was a question he had asked of himself more than once in the weeks since it had all gone down.

She thought about it. "It sounds like not marrying her was the right decision. Happy ending."

Right. Okay, then. A weight he didn't even know he'd still been carrying lifted away from his shoulders.

"And what happened with your mother?" she asked.

"What with the PR disaster brought upon us by my runaway bride, Sadie and I managed to make a deal with my uncle that suited us all better. She promised not to marry me or anyone in my family and he would agree to leave our mothers alone and never to meddle in our love lives again."

A light lit Amber's eyes. "Sounds like a good deal."

"Sadie is a much better negotiator than I will ever be."

"I like the sound of her."

"I believe she'd like the sound of you too."

Hugo hadn't felt the words coming, but as soon as they were said he knew them to be true. Sadie would take one look at Amber and see a kindred spirit for sure. Something unlocked inside him at the thought.

"So you don't have to marry any more?" Amb asked, her voice now more careful.

"I do not." And then he understood the rea

for her care and he felt another door open inside. If he didn't curb the unlocking soon he'd have nowhere left to hide. "I did not latch on to you hoping you might be my next victim, Amber. What happened between us…"

"Yes. Okay. No need to go there."

In the moonlight, this beautiful woman made of fight and fire lying within reach, he wasn't so sure any more.

But Amber went on. "And your mother is now safe. I'm glad for her. It must have been frightening, the prospect of being kicked out of her home for no reason other than the whim of one man."

Hugo went to nod…but caught himself in time. Clever girl. While he'd been trying to figure out ways of getting her to trust him again, she'd just tied him neatly in a big fat knot.

"Ironic, don't you think?" she went on. "That fear for the loss of home sent you rushing to marriage. Yet that is what you plan to inflict on all of us. On me."

His smile was without humour. "Ah, but I did not fear the loss of my home for myself. My connection to the palace is tenuous. I could happily live anywhere. A four-poster bed in Paris. A tent in the Sahara. A hammock slung between two um trees. As, I believe, would you."

He'd said it in jest. But beneath it, like a silthread in a sea of black, it twisted through the night connecting them. Like a language only they knew. Secret stories, stolen moments that belonged only to them.

"So there's really no chance you might one day rule?"

"The succession plan is ancient and twisted. And if you ask Reynaldo, the current uncle in charge, he is going to live for ever." He sat forward on the chair, leaning towards her, now determined to find another way in. "It's just a title, Amber. A side note in my bio that refers to the family into which I was born. Just as you are a Hartley, I am a Giordano."

"Ah, but I was not born a Hartley."

Just when he began to feel comfortable, she knocked him sideways. Yet again. "You weren't?"

"I was born Amanda Grantley. But after I legally divorced my parents when I was sixteen I also changed my name."

"Excuse me, you divorced your parents?" His mind shot back to the rare times he'd been able to get anything out of her about them and all he came up with was lawyers and master manipulators.

"Separated. Emancipated. No longer governed by. Anyway, I picked a name near enough to instinctively respond in answer to it, but still wholly my own. Now it feels like Amanda was a poor sad little girl I once knew."

Sixteen? Hugo had been in boarding schoo

Scotland at sixteen. His father had been gone a year, his connection to the palace now tenuous, his biggest concern how to sneak beer into the dorms. He'd barely been able to make a decision about which socks went with which pants at sixteen. Or what to do about his first crush, his oldest friend Will's sister, Clair. While Amber...

"You were declared an adult by the state. At sixteen."

She nodded. "For all intents and purposes. I was precocious. I had to be. My parents are in demand in the human rights field, and their work keeps them occupied. I was pretty much raised by nannies. When they opened their eyes one day and decided that they quite liked the young woman I had become I was suddenly of interest to them. When they began to bring me out at parties, showing off their daughter like I was one of their Picassos, I took them to court, proved my maturity, and their lack of parental care, and won."

"Hell, Amber."

"I've shocked you a little, haven't I?"

"I'll say."

"Good. I feel ever so slightly like I've just clawed back some ground."

Keep clawing, he thought. Maybe there was chance they could meet back in the middle ce more.

"How long has it been since you saw your parents?"

"I told you, not since I was sixteen. No, I lie. I was working in a bar in Sydney once when they came on the TV. Looking all sanctimonious as they talked about the children they had helped all over the world. I packed up and left. Not long after that I found my way here."

"So we both had a pretty regular upbringing, then?"

"Sure. Only yours had more tiaras." A smile hooked at the corner of Amber's mouth. A razor-sharp sense of humour, and just a little vicious… the way he liked it.

There was something still going on here, between them. Something rich and deep and untapped. If only he knew how to make her see.

She got in first. "One more question, then I will let this be."

"Ask away." The fact that they were talking, really talking, had him feeling better than he had in days.

"Do you wish you could one day be in charge?"

And just like that she cut right to the heart of things. "Once upon a time. But now? I am content with my contribution."

"Which is?"

He pulled himself to sitting, putting his fe to the ground. "I find tracts of royal land n towns that are enduring hardship because their industries—milling, mining, transport—have dried up. Families are struggling to support themselves without welfare. And I build—"

"Resorts. Of course you do." Amber hauled herself upright, her feet hitting the ground as well. Her face sank into her hands.

"I give families jobs; first in construction, then in services. My developments give struggling communities a future."

"Admirable."

"Thank you. I want to turn my mother's home into something workable, useful, beautiful too. To allow it to thrive I will put money into town infrastructure. Shopfronts such as yours can expand. Sunflower and Johnno will have access to top-notch medical attention. It will bring this place alive, giving back to the community that looked after it while my family was gone. It was you who gave me the idea, Amber. You woke me up."

They locked eyes in those few moments, connecting them in ways Hugo wasn't equipped to name.

The last time he'd felt anything close to this he'd been a young man. He'd not long lost his father. Barely able to control his thoughts, much less his hormones, he'd met Clair—Will's twin sister. They'd shared an unexpected summer in llemont while Will was stuck at home in London with a broken leg. He'd barely begun to know her before she'd fallen ill. And succumbed. On top of the loss of his father, the tragedy of losing Clair had emptied him.

For a long time, Clair had been his *what if?*. A valid reason not to get too close.

Until Amber.

Now he knew his attraction to Clair had been forged from limited supervision and adolescence, the memories drenched in the golden glow of youth.

With Amber he was a grown-up.

Those weeks in her shack—the long, lazy days, the soft, warm nights, the talk of nothing, the luxurious quiet—had put him back together in places he'd not even known he was still broken.

Now the world shrank around them. All he could see was Amber; fierce, tough and confused. About him. It was a start, he thought, a way back.

But then she pulled herself to her feet. "Truce over," she said. "Our ten minutes is up."

On his feet now too, Hugo said, "Amber, come on."

She held out a hand, as imperious as any princess he had ever known.

But he took a step towards her. Then another.

She looked spooked. "How dare you suggest the resort idea was my fault?"

"It was absolutely your fault." His next step

brought them toe-to-toe. He hadn't been this close to her in days. The scent of her skin, the power in those eyes—he felt drunk on her nearness.

His voice was rough as he said, "Amber."

He didn't even realise his hand was on her cheek until she leant into it. The feel of her skin after missing it, missing her, for the past few days was like an elixir. His blood, sluggish before then, began to pump in earnest.

Amber pulled away, turning, holding both arms across her belly. "I don't feel good."

"Neither of us feels any good. The way things ended…it feels unfinished. We feel unfinished." His mouth suddenly dry, he pushed past it, knowing he'd never forgive himself if he didn't try. "I never had any expectation of our time together. I still don't. But I miss you, Amber. I miss waking up to find you've stolen all the pillows. I miss watching you dress in your spacesuit. I miss watching you get out of your spacesuit. I miss listening to your voice as you tell stories in the darkness."

Amber shook her head hard. "No, I mean I really don't feel good."

She pushed away from him then, ran to the nearest flowerpot and threw up into a rose bush.

CHAPTER FIVE

AMBER LEANT AGAINST the open door of her bathroom, relishing the feel of the cool wood against her cheek. Whatever had been in Sunflower's stew the night before had not agreed with her. And had continued not agreeing for many, many hours.

In fact, it had been a rough night all round.

After embarrassing herself in the flowerpot, Hugo had insisted on taking her home. But she'd been adamant, telling him she was not about to fall for his plan to muddy her case by being seen coming out of her place in the dark of night.

But the truth was she was mortified beyond belief. The thought of him being nice to her, looking after her, was too much.

She'd gone over there to put her foot down, to insist he make changes, or give up the idea wholesale. Instead she'd come over faint and had to lie down.

And in the quiet that followed, it had felt far too much like before—when talk had been easy, when they'd been...*together*. And then there had been a moment—if a long-drawn-out stretch of breathlessness and anticipation could ever be deemed a mere moment—when the space between the had contracted as if it was being sucked into a black hole.

Throwing up in the bushes had merely been the cherry on the cake.

When Prospero had arrived and Hugo had asked him to escort her in his stead, she'd wept with relief. Literally. And she wasn't a weeper. Just another level of mortification to add to the rest.

But Hugo had taken it in his stride. He'd been kind, protective and supportive. *A true gentleman.*

Her stomach roiled. She closed her eyes, placed a quieting hand on her abdomen and breathed. Maybe it wasn't food poisoning. Perhaps it was a stomach bug. Or—

Amber's eyes flew open and she stared into the middle distance, calculating madly in her head.

No. It couldn't be that.

She crawled back to bed and grabbed her phone, checking the app where she kept track of her periods, before sliding to her backside, extremities numb, sweat prickling all over her skin.

She was a little irregular, could be a few days out, here and there. But even she couldn't justify the great red "negative twelve" glaring back at her, meaning her period was nearly two weeks late.

An hour later, Amber sat on the corner of her bed, with Sunflower holding her hand, the two of them staring at the small white plastic doo-hickey resting on Amber's bathroom sink.

"I'm so sorry," Amber said for the thousandth time.

Sunflower squeezed her hand harder. "Shut up, okay? I'm glad you came to me. I'm happy to be here for this, as I know how terrifying this moment can feel."

Everyone knew. Sunflower and Johnno had been trying to have a baby for years. It was how they'd ended up in Serenity—in the hope a holistic life would make all the difference. Which was why Amber had called, begging one of the dozen pregnancy kits she kept on hand, just in case.

"But if it's good news for me it will only hurt you. Don't pretend. I know how much you want this."

Sunflower turned to her with a smile. "The fact that you'd consider it good news is good enough for me."

Good news.

Amber wondered if she'd used those words simply out of kindness for her friend. It couldn't possibly be how she really felt.

She was a nomad. An anonymous traveller, following her nose. Or she had been until she'd landed here.

Now she had a roof over her head. But Hugo was right—there was a bucket to catch the drip in the roof; air whistled through the walls; a very good blanket and Johnno's potent moonshine had kept her warm through winter.

A person could survive that way. But a baby?

She squeezed her eyes shut and for the hundredth time in half the amount of minutes tried to figure how it might have happened.

She wasn't on the pill—it always made her feel nauseous. But as fast as things had heated up, not once had she or Hugo forgotten to be careful. Meaning that if two little blue lines appeared on that stick, their protection had failed.

But good news?

Sunflower gripped her hand harder. "I'm going to ask, and you can tell me to shut it, but do you know who the…"

Amber nodded.

"Super. And, again, tell me if I'm overstepping, but if I were to hazard a guess, might he be a certain newcomer in our midst?"

Amber's gaze shot to Sunflower to find her sweet face warm and open.

"The sexual tension between the two of you is palpable. The entire town saw it at that meeting. Electric! And, I'm happy to say, contagious. The entire commune is going through a red phase. Johnno and I have been at it like rabbits. While Willow and Tomas are back on for the first time in years, much to Tomas's delight. And—"

Amber held up a hand. "It's okay. I don't need the full run-down. Truly."

Sunflower laughed her fey laugh. "Okay. I just find visualisation helps. You know who the father is, and you clearly have a spark. You think a baby would be good news. All signs point to positive to me." She gave Amber a quick hug, leaning her head on Amber's shoulder. "Come on, baby," she whispered. "You can do this."

Amber looked at the ceiling in an effort to hold back tears as she tried to sort through the mess to see how she truly felt about this.

She had been conceived on purpose and her parents had failed miserably. If she was pregnant, it was very much an accident but that would not have to colour the child's life in any negative way. It would be all about the choices she made next.

Her hands were slippery with sweat, and they shook as she reached out for the indicator.

Time slowed. Her hearing turned to fuzz as blood rushed through her head. She lifted the white stick, turned it around and…

Her brain filled with so many thoughts she couldn't pin them down.

"Amber?" Sunflower called out.

"Hmm?"

"What news?"

Sunflower stood and came to her, looking down at the stick, breathing out a long sigh.

A knock banged so hard at the front door the entire place vibrated, dust falling from a light fitting. And they both coughed and brushed dust from their eyes.

"What am I doing in this place? It's a death trap," Amber said, her throat tight.

Sunflower winced. "I did wonder if you'd ever notice."

"The railing wobbles. The front step is on the verge of snapping in two."

Another knock came and with a snap the door swung open by itself, as it tended to do.

And there stood Hugo, backlit, hand raised to knock, hair tumbling over his forehead in that way that made Amber feel all warm and fuzzy.

"Sorry about the door. I'll fix it, of course. I brought the papers from my lawyers that I promised. And I wanted to see if you were feeling..."

Even with his face in darkness she saw the moment his eyes saw the stick she was holding in her hand.

Sunflower placed a hand on Amber's shoulder. "I'll leave you be, honey. You two have a lot to talk about." She leant in and whispered, "Take it easy on the guy. A man with eyes that dreamy can't be all bad. Hey, Hugo."

Hugo nodded as Sunflower wafted past. He even found a smile. "Sunflower. Lovely to see you."

Sunflower put a hand to her heart and gave Amber a last look.

Then it was just the two of them, together in her shack for the first time since she'd kicked him out.

Well, the three of them. Amber, Hugo and The Stick.

He took a step inside, filling the space with his calm, his strength, the scent of him, so familiar, so delicious. "Is that what I think it is?"

She nodded.

"Are you pregnant?"

She held up the stick in answer.

He tore his gaze away from her to glance at it. "One blue line. No, two. There's a second faint one, right? I don't know what that means. Yes? No? Boy? Twins?"

Despite the tension gripping her every cell, Amber somehow managed to laugh. "Yes, Hugo. It means yes."

He breathed out hard through his nose, and before he had the chance to say anything nausea rose thick and fast in her throat and she spun on her heel and ran to the bathroom, this time taking an extra second to shut the door.

Nothing came up as she had nothing left. Her stomach ached from her spasming muscles. Sweat streaked her hair.

She slowly sat on the floor, shaking, in shock her future a blur.

"Amber? May I please come in?"

She closed her eyes. "I'd rather you didn't."

She listened hard for footsteps but heard none.

"Can I get you anything?" he asked, in that voice of his. Velvet, deep, sure. "Food? Water? A doctor?" A beat, then, "Prospero tells me he helped deliver one of his nephews."

Again she laughed, only this time tears fell freely down her face. "Tell Prospero I won't be in need of his services for a good few months."

A few months and there would be someone in her life *looking* to her for support, food, shelter. And love. Change was coming at her whether she was ready for it or not.

"Amber?" His voice was so close she imagined him sitting on the other side of the door, his head leaning back just as hers was. "May I ask...your intentions?"

Amber closed her eyes. For all the wild and crazy going on in her head right now, she hadn't stopped to think about how he must be feeling. Shocked, sure, but in limbo too, not knowing what she planned to do with this news.

"I'm keeping this baby, Hugo."

She heard the outshot of breath even through the old door. "That's good news."

Good news. Those funny two words again.

"Do you mean that?"

"I believe my brain has gone to its most primal

basic state, and I do not have the wherewithal to say anything but the absolute truth."

"Mmm. I hear that."

A few breaths went by and her tummy seemed to settle. Her nerves too. As if not having to go through this momentous thing alone was a relief.

"Hugo?"

"Yes, Amber?"

"I didn't plan for this."

"I know, *miele*. Neither did I."

A beat, then, "I'm sorry."

"Don't be. Don't ever think you have to be…"

She'd heard the emotion rising in his voice before he'd cut himself off. She swallowed, cringing at the awful taste in her mouth.

Hugo said, "I wish… I wish I knew what to say. To do."

"I don't expect anything of you, Hugo." Ugh. That sounded like a line from a bad teen angst movie.

Then Hugo said something she was sure would haunt her for the rest of her days. "That's always been our problem, Amber, you never have."

Amber's hand went to her belly, only this time not to curb the pain therein. For the pain she felt was higher, deep behind her ribs. "I need some time. To get my head around this. To clean my teeth. To sleep. To recuperate."

It was a good while before he said, "Okay."

She heard him shift from the floor, heard his footsteps echo on her rickety floor. Heard him fiddle with the door until it was properly shut.

Then there was nothing but the sound of her breaths. And the knowledge that, no matter what, she would never be alone again.

Hugo lay on the couch in the library, arm slung over his eyes to block out the sun streaming through the huge windows. His gaze glanced over the paintings on the walls—gum trees and billabongs, red dirt and bushrangers. Alien scenes to anyone who'd never seen Australia.

Summer was in its final throes, bringing with it dry winds and temperatures in the high thirties. Prospero was wilting.

What he wouldn't give to be sprawled out in Amber's hammock.

Amber.

Who was pregnant.

With his baby. At least, he assumed it was his. He hadn't asked.

Of course it's yours. This is Amber we're talking about.

He hadn't said much at all, in fact, his subconscious having switched to basic survival mode. All those years of rigid princely training had come to the fore, forcing any feelings about the news to a watertight box while the diplomat took over.

Yes, Amber. Of course, Amber. Whatever you need, Amber.

When she'd asked him to go, he'd gone. Even though he was pretty sure Amber Hartley had no damn clue what she needed.

As for what he needed… For a man who could schmooze in several languages, negotiate multi-million-dollar developments, he was damn useless at intimate relationships.

His first crush, the lovely Clair, had died tragically not long after they'd met and he'd had no idea how to process that. Thus losing his best school friend—Clair's brother, Will—because he'd been too thoroughly schooled in not showing weakness.

As for Sadie… After his uncle had made it clear he would marry or face the consequences, he'd truly thought marrying his great mate Sadie was a good plan. It would give her and her mother security. Never occurring to him that she might not be so emotionally detached as he, and actually hope to one day marry for love.

Thank the gods she had panicked.

And then had come Amber.

A different kettle of fish from any woman he'd ever dated. Any person he'd ever known.

Sadie had known him her entire life and hadn't realised that beneath his outward confidence, the practised ease, was an emotional wasteland.

Amber had seen right through him from the moment they met. Damaged, deliberately isolated, detached. And still she'd taken him in. Until over the weeks, with her, those darker parts of himself had begun to fade, to seem less irreversible, to heal.

And now he was about to become a father. He had no choice but to leap into the unknown.

Hugo pressed himself to sitting, all the better to think. And breathe.

Thankfully he had time. Months, in fact. Could his plan to leave Serenity be put on hold? He had excellent teams in Vallemont who could manage the Dwell Forest resort that was meant to break ground in the autumn. Maybe.

But that was logistics.

This was far bigger than dates and times on a calendar. He was going to be a father.

A father. Considering the lacklustre examples he'd had in his life, he found himself struggling to know what that really meant.

He loved his younger cousins. He'd taught Kit how to catch a ball, and Kane how to ski. He'd frightened off any number of the older twins' suitors, but he was smart enough to know that being an uncle was wildly different from being a father.

The big question hovering on the edge of his mind since he'd seen those two faint blue lines was what if he, like every other man in the Giordano family, found a way to screw it up?

But this wasn't theoretical. Soon, if everything went as it ought, there would be a baby. A child. He would be that boy or girl's father. And Amber would be its mother.

Somehow, amidst the dark quagmire of disquiet roiling inside of him, that was the one shining light. He might not have a clue what kind of father he would make, but Amber as a mother...?

He'd watched her tend her bees with careful fingers and a calm voice. He'd seen her interact with the townspeople over the last few days—never too busy to stop and listen; to offer advice; to lend a hand; to have a laugh. She drew people to her like a flame.

He'd also watched her stand up to a town council, and a *prince*, in order to protect people she cared about.

She was considerate, serious, presumptuous and fierce.

Hugo could not think of a single person he had ever met who was more qualified for the role of mother.

With it came some other feeling—intangible, slippery, warm. But he couldn't hold on to it long enough to know its name.

Feeling as if he was on the edge of some real

sation that would glue it all together, Hugo started when Prospero cleared his throat.

"We have visitors." Prospero's voice had bite to it, as if he were a Doberman who smelled trouble.

Hugo moved to the window, shifting the heavy brocade curtains aside to find a nondescript black town car had pulled up in his front drive.

A pair of men in dark suits hopped out. Something in the way they moved, slow, careful, on high alert, had Hugo shifting closer to the wall. "The men who attempted the attack on my uncle at the picnic—?"

"Were not dressed in suits, Your Highness."

And paparazzi never drove such clean cars.

One of the men went to the back door of the car and pulled it open. A black high heel with a red sole hit the cobblestones, followed by another. Then, out stepped Hugo's aunt, Marguerite—the wife of Sovereign Prince Reynaldo.

Hugo yanked the curtains closed and snapped out of his daydreams. This was no time for exploring his tender side. He had to have his game face on in order to deal with his aunt.

Hugo was out of the door and down the front steps before the car door shut. "Aunt Marguerite."

Adjusting her face away from the snarky bite of the shimmering summer sun, she offered her cheek for a kiss.

"To what do I owe the pleasure?" Hugo asked,

taking in the sombre bodyguards. Four in total...
meaning the unrest back home was not over and
done with.

"To the fact you seem to have forgotten how to
answer your phone."

Others might falter at his aunt's impressively
imperious tone, but she'd chased him and his
cousins around the backyard with a hose when
they were young enough not to be able to out-
run her. "I told you I was safe, which Prospero
no doubt reiterated in clandestine missives sent
back to the palace."

Marguerite looked at him then, really looked at
him. As if trying to see him as something other
than the half-naked little boy running from the
hose water.

Crickets chirped in the dry grass near by.

"Anyway, welcome to Hinterland House." With
its Italianate yellow stucco, towering conifers,
lead-light windows and neat shrubbery, it could
have been transplanted whole from Tuscany.

Marguerite flicked a speck of red Australian
dirt from her white skirt. "Yes. I have been here
before."

The shocks kept on coming. "When?"

"Reynaldo and I holidayed here with your father—secretly, mind you, as we were not yet married—when he dragged us to this place, claiming
a hankering for peaches. Ironic, that."

Hugo kept whatever retort he might have made to himself. He didn't remember his father well enough to defend him, even if his actions had been defensible. Which they hadn't. Would his child judge his choices as harshly one day?

Hugo put the thought aside. For now. Marguerite was a consummate royal—she could sniff out weakness at a hundred paces.

"It's smaller than I remember," said Marguerite.

"You are such a snob."

"Yes, I am. Now, are you going to invite me in or am I to melt into a puddle in this infernal heat?"

Hugo led his aunt into the house. One of her bodyguards stayed by the car, another at the door, one proceeded to case the house and the other camped out in a spot mirroring Prospero, who hadn't moved from his position by the front door.

"Drink?" Hugo offered. "Something to eat?"

Marguerite had barely removed a glove when she said, "Hugo, this is not a social visit. I am here with news. Three days ago, your uncle died."

Hugo's brain froze. One shock too many. "Which uncle?"

She shot him a look, one that asked that he please keep up. "The Prince. Reynaldo. My husband. The Sovereign Prince of Vallemont."

Only then did he see her hands were shaking, how drawn she looked, the tightness around her eyes. "Marguerite—"

When she saw him coming in for a hug she stopped with a hand. "We have no time for that. It has been three days. There is much to be done."

"Three days?" While he'd been busy at town hall meetings, having cups of strange tea and trying to keep his hands off the local honey-seller, his uncle had gone. What the hell was wrong with his family? The way he'd learned of his own father's demise was staggering in its similarity, tearing open old wounds until anger spilled through him like poison.

"How did I not hear of this? And don't tell me it was because I wouldn't answer my phone. You could have left a message. Email. Overnight mail. You've clearly been in touch with Prospero. What's wrong with you?"

If Marguerite heard the anger in his voice she did not show it. "We could not release the news without letting the people know who their next ruler will be. Officially, he is in bed with the flu, while he is actually in a freezer in the local morgue." She coughed at the end, a gloved fist pressing against her mouth.

Hugo's heart felt as though it had been squeezed.

Everyone in the palace knew that she and Reynaldo had been married in name only for years. They kept separate apartments in the palace—but that was perfectly normal in the royal household.

They also kept separate calendars and engagements—again normal. The fact that she openly detested the man hadn't helped Hugo's views on married life over the years.

Bluebirds and love hearts might not be the theme of their relationship, but they'd had a family. Shared a life. Whoever had led her to believe she had to be stoic at a time like this deserved to be shot.

Whether she wanted him to or not, he moved in and wrapped his arms around her, breathing deeply, encouraging her to do the same. Until her short, raspy breaths matched his and her trembling abated. "Tell me what happened."

"It was awful," she allowed. "Too awful."

"What happened? And the twins? Are they okay?"

"His heart gave way."

"His heart?"

Reynaldo had been a big man with a beard like a Viking's. He'd seemed indestructible. As if he could protect Vallemont by sheer force of will alone. Yet the last time Hugo had seen his uncle he'd been ashen, Hugo's non-wedding having taken its toll. He swore under his breath.

"Do not blame your absence. It was a weak constitution and a lifestyle of excess. The belief he could do it all on his own. He was a Giordano after all." Marguerite smiled with her eyes. "The men in your family have not proven themselves equipped for longevity, delegation or fidelity."

Hugo's eyebrow twitched. The fact he'd just been navel-gazing about this exact concern hit home hard.

"Except for you, of course," said Marguerite, looking at him strangely. "Unless that's why your little friend left you at the altar?"

Hugo stiffened. "It is not."

"No. I wouldn't think so. If our country has any hope of producing a truly admirable Giordano it is you."

Something in Marguerite's tone was beginning to rub against the grain. Hugo ran a hand up the back of his neck and stepped away.

"What did you mean by 'letting the people know who their next ruler will be'?" The members of the royal household were versed in the twisted intricacies of royal succession before they could walk. With Reynaldo and Marguerite's twin boys too young to rule, it fell to Reynaldo's younger brother, Prince Ralph. "Uncle Ralph is married. Of age. And more than capable."

But Marguerite shook her head.

"It has come to our attention that he is not actually married to your aunt, Esmeralda, as she never divorced her first husband. As it turns out, Reynaldo discovered the truth of it a few months ago. Assuming he would live to see his own son grow up and take the throne, he kept it to himself. Yet—"

"The marriage requirement is invalidated." Hugo swore beneath his breath. "So that also means that Jacob—"

"Is a bastard."

Hugo gave his aunt a deadpan stare, but she didn't flinch. "I would not have put it that way. But yes." Meaning the succession of Hugo's other of-age cousin had been nullified in one clerical swipe.

Hugo moved slowly to a window, his gaze unseeing as he looked out on the happy blue sky over Serenity. His voice sounded as though it came to him from another room as he said, "So, unless I am mistaken, you are here to inform me that I am to inherit the throne of Vallemont."

"You sound honestly surprised. Did you not have an inkling? Did you not wonder why your uncle encouraged you to marry our dear Sadie? He wanted you to be ready for this."

Hugo turned on his aunt. "He did not merely *encourage* me to marry Sadie. He blackmailed me into it."

Marguerite's gaze was calm, measured. She came to him, put a cool hand over his. "Watching your father self-destruct pained him. Watching you turn rogue and wander further from the family broke his heart."

"That does not excuse his actions. He threatened Sadie's mother's job. Threatened to throw my mother out of the country."

"This is not about him," said Marguerite, politically savvy to the last. "Not any more."

Hugo ran a hand down his face, scraping against the stubble that had grown back. "And if I refuse?"

"Cousin Constantine."

Hugo's hand dropped. "You are kidding."

Marguerite shook her head. "He's next after you."

"He's eighty-three. And a clown. Literally. I remember him performing at my eighth birthday party. He scared the living daylights out of me."

Marguerite's shrug was as elegant as it was possible for a shrug to be. "Your country is rudderless. And I for one can think of no one better than you to steer the ship."

When Hugo realised he was holding his breath he let it go.

His entire childhood he had been prepared for this moment. When his father had died, the opportunity to put his knowledge, his education, his ideas to use had been snatched from his grasp, sending him spinning out into the world, a royal rebel whose success had been both a revelation and a thorn in his uncle's side.

With his next breath he felt the last vestiges of that rebellion dissolve away.

"I will have my lawyers double-check everything you have told me."

"I'd be disappointed if you didn't."

"And if this turns out to be fact, it will not be announced until I have spoken personally with Kit."

Marguerite raised a single thin eyebrow. "My son is twelve, and mourning the loss of his father."

"That is not all he will mourn. Reynaldo's first-born son was brought up believing that one day he would rule. He has not only lost his father, but also the only version of a future he has ever considered. No one understands the pain of *that* loss more than me."

Marguerite nodded.

"What else needs to be done?" Hugo asked.

"You must return home immediately. The sooner the funeral, the better for the children and stability."

"Agreed. But I would have to return immediately afterwards. I have loose ends that need tying up."

Marguerite made to insist before changing tack. "What could possibly bring you back here?"

Plenty, he realised. In a short space of time he had made real connections, his Australian roots digging in fast. Then there was the resort. And there was Amber. Amber, who was pregnant with his child.

Hugo closed his eyes against what felt very much like a wave of despair. His hope of sticking around, of shifting things in his life to accommodate months of getting to know her, to see if their connection was worth exploring above and beyond the fact they would have a child together, had just been unduly snatched away.

It was time for him to go home.

Marguerite went on, "After which you must marry some lucky girl, and fast. I will write up a list of suitable young women. The coronation will occur right after."

With that, she curtseyed. His venerable aunt, a fierce, battle-hardened woman, bowed before him, and said, "Your Highness."

Hugo rolled his eyes. "Stand up, woman."

She glanced up at him. "Is that a yes?"

He took a deep breath, giving himself one last moment to be sure. But his answer had been written on his heart the moment things had become clear.

"Yes," he said, his shoulder blades snapping together. "My answer is yes. Now, come with me while I find you a drink. And a room. In that order."

"Bless you, dear boy." Marguerite slowly untwisted from her curtsey and slid him an unexpectedly watery smile. "I knew you would turn out to be the very best of them."

"We shall see."

When his aunt was settled—prostrate on a spare bed, snoring quietly, a carved wooden fan pushing the hot air around the room—Hugo headed back to the library to find Prospero still hadn't moved.

Though move he did when he spotted Hugo, bowing deeply, with a deep, proud, "Your Highness."

"Don't feel so punished now, do you, big guy?"

Prospero looked up, his smile wide and full of straight white teeth Hugo had never seen before.

"I need you to do something for me."

"Anything, Your Highness."

Hugo wanted to command the big guy to call him Hugo, but considering the change of circumstances it might give him an aneurism. So he went with, "Stay with my aunt. Let me know the moment she wakes up. There is something I must do alone."

CHAPTER SIX

WHEN AMBER WASN'T to be found in her shack, Hugo went to look for her in the next logical place. Through the cool shade of the patchy trees to the north-east of the shack and then the darker depths of Serenity Forest.

This was where he'd imagined a string of secluded bungalows. Blond wood cladding, slate-grey roofs, muted colours to blend in with as much of the forest as they could save.

When the idea had first come to him, he'd called his uber-designer in Bern. Her response had been "nudes, taupes and creams" with "splashes of mossy green" to "effect an aura of calm, of solace, of rest". The woman could read minds. His dream had been to share the healing magic of this land with as many people as possible. And people would come. People needed a place like Serenity.

Stepping carefully now over fallen logs and random rocks, Hugo came upon her in a small glade.

Long shadows cast by saplings dappled in afternoon light cut across Amber's face, her loose white button-up shirt, her short denim cut-offs. Wild flowers brushed against her bare ankles. Her strangely beautiful dog sat lovingly at her feet.

Hugo kept to the shadows for a moment and took it all in. No wonder his embitterment had crumbled in this place. A person could only take so much light, and life, and exquisite beauty before he had to open up and let it in.

Amber stood by a hive he hadn't seen before. Where the others had been painted every colour under the sun, decorated with smiley faces, cartoony red mushrooms and star fields by Amber's friend Sunflower, this one was clean, white, new.

Bending over, peering into a hole at the front before moving to the back of the hive where she proceeded to attach a hunk of Styrofoam, Amber was tearing strips of tape from the roll with her teeth.

For all the time he'd spent with her—first in the quiet of the cabin and then the white noise of the public arena—the woman was still an enigma. She looked like a French film star. Spoke like a corporate lawyer. Pretended to be a flower child. And acted as though nothing and no one could ever hurt her.

But he'd hurt her. Having picked their relationship apart in his head over the past several hours, he knew that now.

He'd believed her when she'd acted as if her anger towards him was because of the resort, probably because it let him off the hook. But it had been more than that. Deeper. She'd been hurt because she cared. For him. He wasn't the only one whose life had been altered by their time together.

At least, that was what he was counting on. Because if he was wrong, if he was mistaken about her feelings for him, his plan would be defunct.

He ran a hand over his face. The fact that he'd had to choreograph a "plan" at all was less than ideal. If he had the luxury of time, things might be different. Hell, they'd *have* to be different. But none of this was normal. It hadn't been from the very start.

But the bigger truth was that there were bigger things at play now than her feelings. Or, for that matter, his.

A twig snapped, and then Amber bounced about, holding a bare foot.

Which was when Hugo realised something was very wrong.

Amber was tending her bees—meaning she ought to be covered head-to-toe in gloves, veil, overalls and those bright yellow gumboots.

Fear speared his guts like an arrow, panic swelling from the wound. And he was running before he even felt his feet move.

"Amber!" he called, rushing towards her, darting around saplings, waving his arms as if he might be able to distract the swarm before they touched her.

She quickly looked over her shoulder as if a bear might be behind her.

Then she turned to him, shoved her hands on her hips and shouted, "What the hell are you doing?"

"Saving you, you great fool!" Then he swept her into his arms and carried her away, bracing himself for the stings that would pierce his clothes any second. Not caring, as his caveman instincts had kicked in. *Protect woman. Protect child.*

"Let me down!" she said, wriggling like a fish on a boat deck.

"Not going to happen," he gritted out as he avoided getting smacked. And kicked. Bee stings had nothing on her. She was slippery too, sunscreen and sweat making her skin slick.

Hugo gritted his teeth and carried her until she was far enough away that he could be sure she was safe.

The second he stopped she wriggled free and pushed him away. She swept her hair from her face and stared him down. "Are you insane? Has the heat gone to your head?"

"I might ask the same of you." He waved an arm down her body, his gaze catching on the open neck of her shirt and the glimpse of a pink lace bra beneath. He knew that bra. He'd removed it with his teeth. And in the quick glance he saw that he'd left a tear.

Hot, mentally exhausted and turned on, Hugo's voice was a rumble as he said, "Where the hell is your gear, Amber? Are you trying to hurt yourself? And what about the…?"

The baby. He'd yet to say the word out loud. Even thinking it brought up more emotions than he could pin down.

Amber's eyes flickered at the missing word, but she didn't jump in to finish his sentence this time. Instead, she licked her lips, and said, "These are native Australian stingless bees, you idiot. Emphasis on the *stingless*."

"How can you be sure?" he asked. He felt like an idiot as soon as he asked. And yet, if pressed, he knew he'd have asked the same again. His need to protect her outweighed not looking like a fool by a long shot.

And he saw the moment she realised it too.

It was a rare sight, seeing her eyes soften that way. Her already pink cheeks darkening in abashment. He drank it in. Drank her in. She had feelings for him, all right. What he hadn't counted on was his crumbling control over his feelings for her.

"Come on," she said, taking a step towards the hive. Then, rolling her eyes, she grabbed him by the hand and dragged him through the forest.

Ned leapt between them, happy the gang was back together, while Hugo's synapses fired and misfired by turns at how good, how right, it felt to have Amber's hand in his. How much he hoped she wouldn't fly off the handle; that she'd listen to what he'd come there to say.

He curled his fingers tighter around hers. She looked back.

But then she very deliberately let go, her hands tucking together. "Hugo."

"Yes, Amber."

"I'd like you to meet my newest hive. I've been saving up for these guys for months. They're not cheap. But they are so very worth it."

"And stingless?"

"Stingless."

He watched the hive but saw nothing except a small area of tacky black near the opening. But as they stood in the quiet glade he heard the hum. The gentle buzz. And then…there. One. And another.

"They're smaller than the stingy bees so they produce less honey. But what they do produce is delicious with lots of healing properties. But the best bit is that they are amazing pollinators. These little sweeties might just save the world."

Hugo planned to step in and save his country. Amber wanted to save the world.

Then her hand went to her belly and Hugo's world shrank to about two square metres.

"Are you okay?" Hugo asked, stepping in. "Was that pain? Or a…kick?" Hell, he had no clue.

By the flat stare she shot him, she clearly did. "I'm a month along, Hugo. There will be no kicking for some time."

"Then why did you wince?"

"I've been throwing up most of the day. It's left me a little tender, that's all."

"Right," said Hugo.

And Amber gave him a look. A look that connected them. It was the first time they'd spoken with any sense about the fact that they were going to have a child together.

"It may be obvious," said Hugo, "but I've never been in this…situation before."

Her eyebrows shot towards her hairline. "Me neither, thank you very much."

Going on instinct, he took a risk, asking, "Does this all feel as strange to you as it does to me?"

"If you mean you feel like you're living outside of your body and yet are truly aware that you are a living, breathing, cell-duplicating body for the first time in your life, then yes."

"Exactly like that."

In the shade of the hot summer's day, the both of them wildly out of their comfort zones, they burst into laughter.

This woman, he thought. His deep subconscious adding, *Do not let her slip away or I will never forgive you.*

There was a moment when he thought about revealing himself to her, telling her how much he wished they could go back to the ease, the simplicity, the warmth before real life had intervened with such alacrity.

But it was a risk he wasn't willing to take.

He was about to become the sovereign ruler of a country. Every decision he made from here on in would affect the lives of tens of thousands of people.

His only choice in the matter was to leave emotion out of it; to make her an offer she couldn't refuse.

"Amber," he said.

As she heard the serious note in his voice, her laughter dried up. "Yes, Hugo."

"I'm going to say some things now and, before you leap in with thoughts and questions and concerns, I'd like you to let me finish."

She opened her mouth to retort, but he held up a finger. An inch from her mouth. The warmth of her breath rushed over his skin. But he would not be distracted.

"And, once I'm done, I would like to hear your thoughts, questions and concerns. Every single one."

The sass slipped a little then. As if she wasn't

used to being offered the floor. As if she was used to having to fight for it. It was enough for her to acquiesce.

Hugo filled Amber in on the turn of events. And then, "A week ago I was fifth in line to the throne. In a few days I will return home to be crowned the Sovereign Prince of Vallemont."

Amber's hand slipped from her hip to her belly. As well it might. For the second in line to the throne might well be growing inside of her.

To that, Hugo added, "There are certain stipulations that must first be met. I must be of age. Which I am. I must be male—"

She opened her mouth. He held up the finger again. Her eyes crossed as she stared at it, then she closed her mouth.

"—a stipulation which I would hope to change when the job is mine. And I must be married."

At that she stilled. Only her honey-blonde waves shifted in the hot, dry breeze.

"Your turn," he said.

"You're not married, right?" she blurted.

"No."

She breathed out, muttering, "That would have been the real cherry on the cake."

He opened his mouth.

She held up a finger. "My turn."

He closed his mouth.

"There's a strong chance I'm wrong, but I

have a feeling that I know where you are going with this. And I think you should stop now. Before either of us says something we can't take back."

"Marry me."

"Hugo!" Amber paced away a few steps before pacing back again. Ned followed, panting, happily thinking it was a game. "I just said—"

"I don't want to take it back." He stepped in close, took her by the hand—both hands—holding her gaze with everything he had. "Amber, you are pregnant with my child. I will not be an absentee father like mine was to me."

He saw a flicker then. Of understanding. Of empathy.

"I must go home. It's not a choice, it's necessary to the future of my country. To the people of my country. There is only the slightest tinge of arrogance in my stating that I am the best chance they have for a bright, prosperous, safe future. Having you near me, *with* me, when our child is born, is of the utmost importance to me."

He then saw the moment she shut that empathy down. Her head shook side to side. "I can't. Hugo, it's a ridiculous notion. We barely know one another."

"Not true. I know that your parents did not appreciate you. I know that you are fearless, and kind. I know that you doubt yourself at times. And that everyone who knows you respects and admires you."

He hung every hope on the fact that she didn't blink.

"These past few days have been a challenge, but the time we spent together in your shack, talking rubbish, making one another laugh, making love, proves that if we choose to we can get along just fine."

She swallowed, her gaze dropping to his mouth, and he wondered if her vision of "getting along" matched his.

"That does not mean I am under any illusion that our relationship will ever be that way again." Only then did he realise how much he wanted it to. But no, now was not the time to speculate. "You would be made comfortable. You would have your own apartment within the palace. You would have complete freedom to do as you please. You could rule at my side or in name only. You could champion any cause that speaks to you, with the backing of a royal name, royal funds, royal gravitas. And our child will have a family. A mother and a father."

"Hugo," she said, her voice a whisper, and he knew he was giving her more than he'd intended. But the words were coming from some place real. And raw. And open. And, while fighting with her had been fun, this felt far better.

But he knew it would be short-lived. For he hadn't played his trump card yet.

He reached up and tucked a swathe of hair behind her ear, relishing the feel of her, the warmth of her, for it might well be the last time she let him this close ever again.

"One more thing."

Gripped now, discombobulated by the ridiculous drama of it all, her voice was barely a whisper as she said, "What on earth else could there be?"

He looked into her eyes, remembering what it felt like to fall into the bright whisky depths as she fell apart in his arms, and said, "If you agree to come with me, marry me, be my Princess, and raise our child in the Palace of Vallemont, I will give up the plans to turn Hinterland House into a resort."

And like that the brightness went away as her eyes narrowed. A crease appeared above her nose. And she let go of his hand.

"Hinterland House has been in my mother's family for generations, so I will save it for my children, our children, as well as five acres to the west. But I will gift the rest of the land to the town of Serenity. Including the lavender fields, the forest...and I will sign over your hill to the commune."

Amber swallowed hard, even as a tear ran

slowly down her cheek. She quickly swiped it away.

He wished he could take her in his arms, run a hand down her back, over her hair. Kiss away those tears. Kiss her until she sighed. Until they both forgot what the hell they were even talking about.

He'd had no idea how hard this would be. How physically brutal. It actually hurt. Deep inside his chest. But with the future of his beloved country at stake and a child on the way, he did not see that he could have gone about it any other way.

"I don't expect you to make a decision right now. But time is pressing. I am heading home immediately for my uncle's funeral. I will be back in time for the town meeting. I will need to know your decision by then."

A shiver rocked her body and she seemed to snap back to her old self, her eyes flashing, her fists curling into hard balls. It was far easier to handle than the tears.

"My decision?" she hissed. "Let me get this straight. If I agree to marry you…" she stopped to swallow the words "…and move to the other side of the world, raise the baby I only found out I was having today, in a palace, then you will not tear down my friends' homes. But if I say no then you will go ahead with the plan to build your resort. Just because you can."

"Yes."

She breathed out through a hole between her lips. Her eyes were bright, her face was pale and she was glorious. This woman to whom he had just proposed. Who, no matter what happened from here, would never fully trust him for the rest of her life. Hugo soaked in the sight of her like a man on his way to prison.

"I knew you were a bender of the truth. I knew you kept things close to your chest. Until this moment I had no idea you were an asshole."

Hugo kept his cool by reminding himself his family had not prospered for as long as they had by being the nice guys. "I'd rather think of my offer as knockout negotiation."

"I bet you would. This isn't normal, Hugo. You do realise that?"

He ran a hand through his hair, his cool hitting breaking point. "We have never been normal, Amber, not from the moment we met. We ended up in bed before we even knew one another's names. Time lost all meaning as we lost ourselves in one another. I had no idea what day it was, what date, whether it was morning or afternoon. It didn't matter. I can't presume to know what it meant to you, Amber, but for me those weeks…"

Too much. The moment he caught her eye again, he knew he'd said too much.

But then Amber breathed, the air shaking through her like an earthquake. And he knew it had been as transformative for her as it had been for him.

And he knew, in that moment, how to get the answer he wanted.

He had one chance to get this right. It was off plan, and risky as all hell, but he went for it.

Reaching out to her, Hugo took her hand and gently pulled her into his arms, an inch at a time. Her hands moved to rest against his chest but she didn't push him away. She was listening now.

"Amber, every person I have ever met has seen me as a prince first and Hugo second. But for those weeks, with you, I was simply a man. You were short with me if I was presumptuous. You were cool with me if I made you angry. You didn't laugh if my jokes weren't funny. You berated me if I made you wait. And I wouldn't give up a second of it."

He dropped his hand to her side then, his thumb resting against her belly. Beneath that warm skin his child was growing, a child created during one of those meandering days—or one of those decadent nights.

"Not a single one."

He'd meant to leave it there, but having her in his arms again, swamped in memories of their time together, he found he couldn't let her go. He pulled her closer still and she let him. Then, before he could stop himself, he leaned down and he kissed her.

In the back of his mind he imagined the moment as a place-holder, a precursor to the official sealing of a deal.

But muscle memory took over and soon his hands were in her hair; hers gripping his shirt for dear life. And the kiss took on its own life, pulling him under. Deep. His heart thundered hard enough to burst.

His senses reeled. Shadow and light played on the backs of his eyelids. The taste of her was sweet and fresh and familiar. Her softness gave under his touch.

Heaven and hell. Wanting her, while knowing that if he had her it would be due to a devil's bargain.

As if remembering the same, she broke the kiss. Sighing as her lips left his.

Their foreheads touched for just a moment, before Hugo lifted his head and found her eyes. Whisky-brown. Flecked with sunshine and gold. And trouble.

"Think about it," he said, his voice rough. "Whatever you decide I will accept your answer unequivocally. The next town meeting. Let me know your answer by then."

And then he let her go, aching at the way she had to catch herself, as if her knees had gone soft.

Then he turned and walked back through the forest, seeing nothing. It was a miracle he didn't walk into a tree.

The sweet warmth of her body was imprinted on his. The honeyed taste of her lips still flowing like hot treacle inside him.

His head hurt at what he had just done. His gut burned. Even his bones throbbed.

Was this how Reynaldo had felt when he "encouraged" him to marry Sadie, blanketed by his sureness that it was the right thing to do?

Was this what it meant to rule?

If so, Hugo knew he shouldn't be so concerned about getting through with his heart intact. He'd be lucky to get by without destroying his soul.

Three days later Amber stood at the podium in front of the town council.

She'd sucked on a lemon just before coming out, so the nausea was at about a four rather than its usual nine or nine and a half. The lights glaring down on her made her head hurt.

Though perhaps that might have had more to do with the fact that her time was up. She had a decision to make that would change her life, and the lives of the townspeople, no matter which way she went.

She glanced over her shoulder at her cheer squad. Sunflower waved and Johnno gave her a thumbs up. Looking at them, she wondered if she ought to have confided in them. Asked their opinion. But she was so used to relying on no one but herself, she'd had no clue where to start.

Raising a child here with these good people would be magical. But if she stayed, the commune would no longer exist, not in the form it kept now, so that made the option redundant.

Also, and this was the thing that had kept her awake at night, no matter how she had come to care for them, they weren't her family. People came, and people went. The ebb and flow of the commune's population was what kept it so vibrant.

On the other hand—there was Hugo. And grrrr, she was so mad at him right now! Madder than she'd ever been at anyone in her entire life—her parents included, which she hadn't thought possible.

Meaning she'd had no choice but to think about why that was.

Sure, his marriage proposal had amounted to extortion. But he hadn't *had* to offer to give up the resort. For all the sangfroid he'd shown making his proposition, she understood he was offering a sacrifice to balance her own.

It was the sentiment that confounded her. He'd

said that being near his child was of the utmost importance, and that he would never be an absentee father. As if he knew exactly how to rip right to the heart of her. Unless, of course, he'd been telling the truth.

Then there was the kiss. It had come from nowhere. Yet at the same time it had been brewing for days.

For a little over three weeks she had experienced the closest thing to comfort she had ever known; waking with Hugo's arm draped over her, protective and warm; falling asleep with him caressing her hair; listening to the deep hum of his voice as he'd chatted to Ned.

She let her gaze drift to the far corner of the room, where Hugo stood with Prospero a hulking shadow at his back. They were mobbed, the centre of a dozen conversations. And yet Amber could feel Hugo's attention attuned to her.

Her tummy fluttered at the sight of him. Nausea. That was what that feeling was.

And anger. Because she was mad at him still. Deeply, hotly mad.

The gavel struck and Amber looked to the front table. Her heart hammered against her ribs. Her vision began to blur.

Before Councillor Pinkerton could call the meeting back to order, Amber held up a finger. "May I beg a minute?"

The councillor looked towards Hugo's corner. "We can spare two."

On unsteady feet Amber turned and walked towards the side glass doors. She waggled a finger at Hugo, motioning for him to follow her.

Outside she paced, the long skirt of her loose dress catching around her ankles every time she turned.

Hugo slid through the door, looking ridiculously handsome with his sexy stubble and his hair falling across one eye. In jeans and a jacket this time, he reminded her far more of the man she'd known than the man he'd turned out to be.

He looked tired, no doubt thanks to flying to the other side of the world and back in the past few days. Burying his uncle. All the while not knowing what her answer might be.

Or maybe it had never really been under contention. Maybe it had always been about giving her time to pretend she had a choice.

"Ned," she croaked. And tried again. "What about Ned?"

"What about Ned?" he said, the first time she'd heard his voice in days.

"He's not mine. Not officially. He was a stray. And he sort of…got attached to me."

"I know the type."

She shot him a look, felt the heat of his gaze slice through her like a knife through butter. "I should leave him behind. This place is all he knows. And what with his hearing…" She flapped her hands, which were suddenly going numb. Her toes were too. She closed her eyes and wriggled her toes.

She felt Hugo take her by the elbows. "Breathe, *miele*. Just breathe. I simply assumed he'd be coming with us. That is what you want, isn't it?"

Amber swallowed. "But what about Customs? Don't you need a vet check? Or immunisation records? Proof he's not going to infect your entire country with some weird Australian disease?"

Every word became harder to come by. She glared at Hugo and felt a little better. Though her righteousness would feel better still if he acted more like an ogre while holding her to ransom. If he'd blackmailed her for profit, not for good. If his super-prince sperm hadn't managed to break through every protection she'd put in place.

"I vouch for him," he said, with a very European scowl. "What is the point of being Sovereign Prince if one cannot take advantage every now and then?"

"Do you mean that?"

"Of course. I plan on taking advantage wherever and whenever I can."

"No, I…" A beat, an unexpected smile, then she said, "You're kidding."

"Much of the time. I have spoken to the relevant authorities already, as I am also thorough."

Amber's thought went to her belly. Didn't she know it?

"Are you ready to go inside? If not I can take your place. I can give the council the news, whatever it may be."

Amber shook her head. "I started this. I'll finish it." But she didn't move.

She looked up, made sure he was looking at her, really paying attention, when she said, "I don't want my baby to be raised by nannies. Or governesses. Or to go to boarding school. Or to sleep in another wing of the palace. I want him or her sleeping with me, if that's what works. I want to carry her and cuddle her and take her everywhere I go. And if anyone—anyone—suggests otherwise, I reserve the right to tell them to back the hell off. No committee. No PR agency. Every decision, whether it is the kind of foods she will eat, or the friends she has, will be up to us, and us only."

She'd been entirely ready to say "me" and "I". But as she looked into Hugo's solemn eyes it had come out "we". For they would be in this together. For real.

She expected him to make some kind of quip to lighten the mood, but he placed a hand on her cheek, looked deep into her eyes and said, "What level of hell did your parents put you through, *miele*?"

She flinched. "I don't know what you—"

"Amber."

She swallowed. "Enough."

He said, "If that is what you wish then that is the way it will be. You have my word."

She nodded. Then, without another word, she went back inside and gave the council the news.

The resort was no longer in play. The commune was saved.

And she was leaving town.

CHAPTER SEVEN

IT HAD ALL happened so fast.

Amber's pregnancy.

His uncle's death.

The trip home for the funeral. The hand-picked interviews announcing his upcoming succession. The chance to fulfil the destiny he had grown up believing would be his.

A very fast visit to see Sadie and her new fiancé, his old friend Will, who had brought him back to earth.

And then back to small-town Australia to get his bride. And to officially remove his resort plans from council consideration.

Used to working by the seat of his pants, he'd taken each revelation and rolled with it.

Only now, in the dark quiet of the private plane, the ocean sliding beneath them with a half-finished glass of Scotch in his hand, did Hugo have the chance to unpack the enormity of what had happened.

He *had* the chance, but he chose not to take it. Instead he twisted his Scotch back and forth, hypnotised by the play of light in the golden liquid.

Sovereign Prince. Father. Husband.

Husband. Father. Sovereign Prince.

Closing his eyes, he lifted the drink and downed it in one go. Wincing as the heat burned the back of his throat.

"Hey."

Hugo looked up, saw Amber leaning in the doorway. Her hair was up in a messy bun and the colourful crocheted blanket she'd used to have on the end of her bed was wrapped about her shoulders. Her eyes were puffy from sleep.

"Are you drunk?" she asked.

"Not yet."

"Is this something I need to worry about?"

Hugo laughed, running a hand up the back of his neck. "Not at all. I was raising a quiet glass to my uncle."

"It looked like you were drowning your sorrows."

"Same thing, I would think."

"Mmm."

Hugo shook off the funk, quickly moving the paperwork he had piled up on the chair opposite his. "Sorry, come in. Sit."

"What's all that?"

He readied himself to brush it off as "nothing", before remembering Marguerite's assertion that the men in his family had not proven themselves equipped for longevity, delegation or fidelity. He had no problem with the third, and the first was out of his hands. But the ability to see and use the resources at his disposal? That was his bag.

Amber was an outstanding natural resource. It would behove him to start as he meant to go on.

"Details of coronation plans," he said, pointing to the document printed on Marguerite's letterhead. "Articles of law currently before parliament. The notebooks are Reynaldo's private records. If there's anything you're keen to have a look through, feel free."

She blinked at him and shook her head. But after a beat she moved to sit in the chair across from his.

"Everything okay?" he asked. "Do you need food? There are more blankets...somewhere. The staff are all over that. Shall I call someone?"

She laughed softly, then pressed a fist over a yawn. "I'm fine. Just...antsy, I guess." She curled her feet beneath her. "You looked to be in deep thought just now. Took me a couple of tries to get your attention."

"I have things on my mind."

"You and me both." A beat, then, "Anything you'd like to talk about?"

"With you?"

"No, with the seatbelts. Yes, with me!"

"You must understand my shock. You've shown an aversion to talking about anything more personal than the weather up until now."

She quelled him with a look. "I'm exhausted. It's messing with my equilibrium. I probably won't even remember this conversation in the morning." She sank down deeper into the chair and let her eyes drift closed. "But sit there and stew. See if I care."

Hugo shifted in his seat, leaning an elbow against the arm rest, balancing his chin in his fingers of one hand. Was she serious? Or pulling his leg? Only one way to find out.

"I was thinking about my aunt and uncle. About what it was like for them when they first found themselves in our position."

Her eyes fluttered open.

"Unlike our exuberant expectation, Reynaldo and Marguerite started their family late. After trying for some time they fell pregnant to much rejoicing all over the land. Then they had twin girls."

"Alas."

"Reynaldo's thoughts exactly. Three years later? Another set of twin girls."

Amber's eyes sparked. "I'm starting to like this story. Still no heir for poor blackmaily Reynaldo. Go on."

"He was beginning to feel punished."

"And why wouldn't he?"

"Our succession laws are ancient and complex, and certainly different from other Royal houses of Europe. Like a house given extensions in different architectural styles over centuries until it no longer makes sense as a building. But there it is, filled with people."

Amber snuggled a little deeper into the chair and leant her head against the leather seat, her eyes sleepy but engaged. And so he went on.

"Growing up, my father was second in line. Charismatic, roguish, larger than life."

"Sounds familiar."

"Ah. But my father's behaviour declined, making it abundantly clear that he wasn't interested in the role of Sovereign and could not care less about playing the part of dutiful public servant. Meaning that, unless Reynaldo had a boy, I was next in line to the throne."

Amber watched him carefully now. Taking in every word. "And then?"

"My father died. I can't even remember much of that time. Flashes of pain. And anger. Mostly anger. For it was a one-two punch. Not only had he left my mother and me for ever, but also with his death I lost my place in the line, relegated down back behind my uncle and his sons. Reynaldo insisted I could still be of use. But I wasn't interested. I gave up on the family and put my energies into other pursuits. And succeeded.

"Reynaldo was not happy. He made life as difficult as possible for my mother as punishment. I

never forgave him for that. And he never forgave
me for walking away."

"My, what a twisty family you have."

"You have no idea."

"Apple doesn't fall far from the tree though,
does it?"

Hugo looked up, his whole body tight. "Excuse me?"

But she didn't back down. The look in her eye
was sharp. And unforgiving. "Don't you see that
you pretty much used the exact same move to get
me on this plane?"

"That's not what I—"

"*Marry me or else I'll tear down your home*?
What would you call it?"

Hugo ran a hand over his face.

"Relax. It's done now. I'm too tired to go another round tonight. So I'm giving you a free pass.
A one-time deal. And only because I can't see
how any normal person could take the amount
of stuff that has been thrown at you in the past
few days and glide through with ease and grace.
It's a lot."

Sovereign Prince. Father. Husband.

Hugo blinked. "It is rather. And I fear there's
more to come. I did some press when I came
home earlier in the week but I didn't stay long
enough to see how it played out. After the wedding that never happened, and my recent extended

absence, I'm not sure how the people will take to a 'rebel prince' as their sovereign."

"What do you imagine they'll do? Protest? Picket? Riot?"

He turned to her with a gentle smile. "You'll find we are a seriously civilised nation. Protests would likely be more in the order of satire. Snarky journalism. A lower than usual crowd at the coronation."

"Wow. Harsh. Brace yourself."

"Quite. It's not violence I'm concerned about. It's ambivalence. We are a proud country and rightly so. It would…sadden me to know I'd had a hand in depleting that civic spirit."

"But that's not the only reason." Her feet dropped to the floor and she leant forward, elbows on thighs, hands falling gracefully over her knees. "You present as if you don't care about all that much—with your slow walk, easy smile, and always with the wry humour. But when you talk about Vallemont you become a different man. This place is truly important to you, isn't it?"

He breathed out hard. "It's who I am."

"And you want to do a good job and look after your people fairly, equitably."

"Yes."

"Then you will."

"You can't possibly know that for sure."

She looked him dead in the eye then. And said,

"I've seen you at your worst now, Hugo. And I've seen you when you're on song. You can do this thing blindfolded and with one hand tied behind your back. And if I can get past my stubbornness to admit I think you won't suck, then it must be true."

He thought he'd believed it too, but hearing her say it with such conviction, for the first time it felt real. Do-able. As if the challenge wasn't overwhelming, but his for the taking.

A smile started down deep before tugging at his mouth. "Will you write my coronation speech? Truly. That was beautiful."

"You bet." She nodded. "And you can do something for me in return. Don't you dare pull any more of that Reynaldo-style rubbish on me ever again, or I'll take it all back. Every word."

"I won't."

"Say it."

"I promise."

"Okay, then." She yawned. "What time is it?"

"Where?"

"Good point."

She pressed to her feet and padded back through the doorway, shooting him one last pink-cheeked smile before she was gone.

"Hot damn," Hugo said, feeling as if he'd been let off the hook and given the greatest gift of his lifetime all in one go.

He sat back in his seat and looked out of the window, at the blanket of stars covering the dark night sky, finally ready to take on whatever came his way.

They flew into Vallemont under shadow of night.

After more than twenty-four hours in the air, constant nausea, close proximity to a man who made her twitch and itch, as well as having to deal with the enormity of what awaited her at the other end, Amber was ready to claw her way out of the plane.

Instead, she allowed the flight attendant to heave open the plane door. Then shivered at the icy air that slithered into the breach, up her legs and into her very bones.

The private airfield was quiet bar the driver of a serious-looking town car with blacked-out windows; engine humming, its exhaust fumes created clouds in the cold air.

Hugo pressed a gentling hand to the small of her back and her skin tingled in response. Not his fault. That kind of thing was bound to happen when she'd agreed to marry a wildly handsome, deeply sexy, powerful man who had swept her off her feet to rescue her from a swarm of stingless bees. *Marriage.* That felt even more strange to her than the fact she would live in a palace and become a princess.

"Everything okay, *miele*?" he asked.

Amber swallowed. The endearment he'd started using screwed with her feelings. But if she called him on it he'd know she *had* feelings. It was a Catch-22.

"Amber, look at me."

She did.

"I meant it when I said you can change your mind at any point. I've been jilted at the altar once already, remember, so if it happens again I'll take it in my stride." He smiled then, as if he did mean it. But she had seen the strain around his eyes. The Furrows of Important Dreams had become permanent the past few days.

Handsome, sexy, powerful and selfless. The guy genuinely wanted to be a good servant to his public. She was in big trouble.

But resist she would. To surround her baby with family it would be worth it.

She shook her head. "I'm fine. Just tired."

"Of course. Let's get you to bed."

Amber closed her eyes for a moment, trapping behind them the plethora of images his words brought forth.

Think of the baby. This is all for her. Or him. Or them. Twins were in the family after all. What have you let yourself in for?

Hugo led her down the stairs and towards the car. Once the bags were squeezed into the boot,

Prospero sat up front with the driver and began speaking animated Italian, leaving Hugo and Amber in the back.

Leaving behind the last throes of Australian summer, they'd hit the end of Vallemontian winter. Through the window, neatly tapered evergreens lined the roadside, mist reflected off glassy lakes, and, framing it all, craggy, snow-dusted mountains created an eerie, otherworldly feel to the place.

"Is that a village up ahead?"

"Not quite yet." Hugo glanced out of the window to check out the lights she'd seen. "It shouldn't be. Not yet."

But then the lights brightened, and she realised they were coming from the side of the road. First sporadically and then in clumps. "Hugo?"

"I see it." He pressed a button in a panel in the back of the limo. "Prospero?"

"Yes, Your Highness."

"The lights?"

"We were given forewarning, Your Highness, hence the armoured car."

Armoured? She reached her hand along the seat until it found Hugo's. He curled it into his warm grip in an instant.

"Should I be worried?"

Hugo opened his mouth to answer but Prospero got there first. "It's the people. They are lining the street, carrying lanterns which they have been making in all the local schools for days. They've come out to welcome you home."

"But it's three in the morning," Hugo said under his breath, as the groups on the side of the road got deeper and deeper the closer they got to a village. Streamers began to float over the car, sliding off the windows. And it had begun to rain what looked like rose petals.

Hugo rolled down the window, against Prospero's protests, and the noise of the crowd intensified tenfold. When he waved, the faces swimming through the darkness beamed and cheered and sang.

Amber laughed, the sound catching on the chilly air pouring into the car and floating away. "And you were worried they might pillage."

Hugo looked at her, surprise and delight etched into his handsome face. He brought her hand to his mouth and kissed it. Hard. Several times. Until she couldn't stop herself from beaming. As for the first time since this whole debacle had begun she realised it might actually be rather amazing.

"Amber?"

"Mmm?" Amber opened her eyes to find she'd fallen asleep. Her head rested on Hugo's shoulder. His arm was around her; his fingers smoothing her hair, distractedly, as if he'd been doing so for some time.

She gently disentangled herself from his arms, and surreptitiously scrubbed her fingers through her hair to get rid of the feel of him. Or maybe not so surreptitiously, as he laughed. His eyes were dark and loaded with understanding.

She looked away to find they'd pulled up outside a crumbling old building dripping with bougainvillea. Moonlight shone against an exoskeleton of scaffolding that seemed to be holding it together.

"Wow," she said. "I didn't imagine the palace to be so…quaint."

"We're not at the palace."

"We're not?"

Hugo grinned. He actually grinned. It reminded her of how he was before.

Careful, commanded the voice in her head. He might be a fixture in her life, which meant amity was more sensible than animosity, but this was an arrangement, not a relationship.

"This used to be a hotel called La Tulipe, but is now the headquarters of the new Royal Theatre, of which I am the lucky patron. Before throwing you on the mercy of the palace, I thought we'd spend our first night with friends."

"Friends?"

Before she'd even got the word out, the car door

was whipped open and with the gust of icy air came a redhead in a pink beanie with a pom-pom on top.

"Hugo! You're late," she said in a lilting sing-song accent that reminded Amber of Hugo's. "It had better be because you stopped on the way for chocolate. Or wine. Or both." Then she leaned down to peer deeper into the car. As she spied Amber, her face broke out into a grin. "You must be Amber. I'm so happy you're here! Oh, Hugo, she's gorgeous. Why did you not tell us how gorgeous she was?"

"Maybe he doesn't think I'm gorgeous," Amber said, then regretted it instantly. "Forget I said that. Jet lag and catnaps, summer to winter—my brain has clearly not found its feet. Hi, I'm Amber."

"Sadie." Sadie grabbed her by the hand and all but dragged her out of the car, meaning she had to climb over Hugo, hands and elbows trying not to land anywhere precarious.

When their eyes locked for a split second he gave her the kind of smile that made thought scatter, bones melt, and strong women rethink their boundaries.

Amber spilled from the car and landed in a Sadie hug that squeezed the air from her lungs so fast it puffed out in a cloud of white. "I am so happy to meet you. You have no idea."

Sadie pulled back, looked into Amber's eyes

and laughed. "Oh, no. What has Hugo said about me? It had better have been nice. For I have stories I can tell you—"

"Leo," said Hugo, now standing very close behind Amber. "It might surprise you to know that Amber and I haven't actually spent all our time together talking about you."

Sadie poked out her tongue and Hugo laughed.

Interesting. From the little that Amber had heard about this woman she hadn't imagined her to be so lovely, so charismatic and warm, Or for Hugo to be so easy with her after what she had done. But if Sadie was indeed a friend of Hugo's it only made sense.

Sadie looked from Amber to the man standing over her shoulder before a smile settled on her face. "You must be exhausted. Let's get you lovebirds inside. Prospero, you have the bags. Excellent. Follow me."

And then she was gone, Prospero in her wake.

"Wait," said Hugo when Amber went to follow. Taking her by the hand and drawing her close. "Don't let her run over the top of you."

"Excuse me?"

"I can see your mind ticking over. Trying to figure her out. Trying to figure *us* out. Leo—Sadie—is my very oldest friend. Which is why I am allowed to say that she is hyperactive, full of energy and opinions and a compulsive need to make everyone around her happy. I know you need your space, your quiet time. Don't be afraid to tell her to stop."

He knew she needed space. He knew she needed quiet time. He knew her.

Determined not to let him know how touched she was, how much that meant, Amber lifted her chin and said, "Do I look afraid?"

The hint of a smile. Then, "No."

"Okay, then."

"It's just… You got me to thinking on the plane. I don't want us to be like my aunt and uncle, so cold with one another they could barely make eye contact. I hope we can be better than that. Because we have a chance to do good here. Together. I am on your side, no matter what Sadie, or Will, or Aunt Marguerite, or the press, or ex-girlfriends who will no doubt come out of the woodwork have to say."

He reached up and pressed her hair behind her ear—a move that always sapped her breath.

Needing to hold on to her dignity before she did something stupid like fall for him, right then and there, in the moonlit darkness, she said, "You don't need a speech-writer, Hugo. You're a natural."

His face split into a smile. "Am I, now?"

"The way you put words together? I have chills."

"Then how's this for a speech? You know I think you're gorgeous, right?"

The cautious voice in her head threw its hands out in surrender. "Hugo, that was a stupid quip. Forget I ever said it."

"Can't. It's out there now. You are gorgeous. But above and beyond that you are smart. Canny. And generous to a fault."

Amber pinched her leg to try to stop the trembles rocketing through her that had nothing to do with the cold. "You promised you wouldn't mess with me."

"On the contrary. If you were not aware of how much I appreciate your decision to accompany me, how much I appreciate you, then I have been remiss. And I apologise."

Desperate to get out of this conversation, she mumbled, "Apology accepted."

No such luck. Hugo moved closer, his voice dropping, the chill in the air nothing compared to his body heat, making her feel all warm and soft and molten. "Now it's your turn to say something nice about me. Quid pro quo."

She laughed despite herself. Better that than sighing, which was what her entire body was on the verge of doing. "My mother always said if I didn't have anything nice to say, not to say anything at all."

"From memory it's been quite some time since you've done anything your mother told you to do."

He was right. Damn him.

And as she looked into his eyes the memory of their first kiss swarmed over her. It had been inside her kitchen, mere moments after she'd invited him inside after finding him in her hammock. Like two lost souls desperate for warmth, for connection, finding recognition in one another's loneliness, they'd fallen together. After which they'd burned up the sheets.

Then something unexpected had happened over the days and weeks. The heat had expanded, allowing for warmth, loneliness giving way to comfort, to small acts of kindness and caring.

Whatever had gone down between them since—the white lies, the disagreements, the forced intimacy neither had asked for—that time had happened. It was a part of their story. A part of them.

Her hand fluttered to his chest to push him away. Or perhaps to give in to the feelings messing her up inside. To take a chance, and risk it all.

"Get a room!"

Hugo blinked, and came to, turning and smiling in the direction of the deep male voice behind Amber. "Will Darcy. Impeccable timing as always."

"Come on, mate. It's bloody freezing out here."

As the men bantered, relief and regret whirled inside of Amber, and she had to grip Hugo's shirt to keep herself from collapsing under the combined weight.

Once she felt able, she turned to meet Hugo's friend Will, a Clark Kent type, with curling dark hair, a cleft chin and bright, clever eyes.

He stepped forward. "You must be the famous Amber. Will Darcy. Pleasure to meet you."

She took his hand and was hit with a wave of familiarity.

"Have we met?"

"I'm sure I'd remember." A smile. Neat white teeth. Dimple in one cheek. English accent. Again those bright, clever eyes.

Then it hit her. She clicked her fingers. "You spoke in a documentary I saw once. You're an astronomer, right?"

He nodded, and held out both hands as if to say, *Sprung.*

"I can't believe this. I was travelling at the time and you were so inspiring I actually decided on my next destination by following the Southern Cross. It's how I ended up in Serenity in the first place. Wow! Ha! This is amazing."

From behind her Hugo grumbled, "She was far less excited when she found out I was a prince."

Will laughed. "Smart woman." He then took her hand, placed it into the crook of his elbow and swept her away from Hugo, through a set of glass doors and inside the building, where they had to dodge drop-cloths and paint buckets.

In the low lamplight she saw crown mouldings, ancient wallpaper and more crumbling brick. It was like something out of a play.

They followed the sound of Sadie's voice to find her regaling Prospero with tales of refurbishment and *Much Ado About Nothing*.

Sadie looked up and saw Amber just as she yawned. "You poor love. Your rooms are right here. One each if you're sticklers for tradition, or share and share alike. Apologies that they are not yet finished. We are a work in progress."

Amber's thank-you was lost in another yawn.

Then Sadie's eyes darted to Amber's belly, before darting away.

And all the good, warm, mushy emotions she'd been feeling towards Hugo evaporated.

He'd told Sadie about the baby. Who else? Did the entire royal family know it was a shotgun wedding?

It doesn't matter, she tried to convince herself. *This was an arrangement, not a relationship.*

"Okay," said Sadie, "we'll head upstairs and leave you to it. Though I'll be fast asleep in two minutes flat, Will will be on the roof looking at his stars if you need anything. Oh, wait." She reached into the pocket of her gown and gave

Hugo a small box. "That thing you wanted me to procure."

"Right. Thanks."

Will took Sadie by the hand and tucked her in behind him. "With that we'll take our leave. Goodnight. Sleep tight. See you when it's light." Then he pressed her ahead of him and into the darkness.

"If you don't have a preference I'll take the room on the left."

"Fine," said Hugo, spinning the box in his hand.

"Anyway, goodnight."

"Wait." Hugo put the box in his upturned palm and held it out to Amber, all remnants of playfulness gone. "I apologise in advance."

Amber took the box, opened it slowly and her jaw literally dropped when she saw what was inside.

It was a ring—a baguette half the size of her pinkie finger set with dozens of different-sized pink diamonds on a thick rose-gold band. "Is this for real?"

"I'm afraid it is. For that is the Ring of Vallemont. Handed down through the family for generations. My grandmother gave it to me after my father died. Quite contentious within the family, as usually it is given to the next in line to the throne. The woman was clearly psychic. When Reynaldo and Marguerite had the boys, I should have passed it on, but for some reason I couldn't. Funny, that."

"Well, it's big. And shiny. And very pink." She went to hand it back.

"No, Amber. It's yours."

"Excuse me?"

"It's your engagement ring."

She looked down at the ring again, this time with a different eye. It was huge. Cumbersome. Like something you saw in a museum, not something you wore for the rest of your married life. "But it must be worth millions."

"No. It's priceless."

She opened her mouth to protest but Hugo shut her down.

"Amber, I know my proposal was not…normal."

"Enough with the normal already."

"Yes. But no matter the circumstance, a woman should at least be given the respect of tradition."

In the near-darkness, it took a moment for Amber to realise Hugo was making to get down on one knee. But Amber grabbed him by the shoulders and yanked him back to standing, her heart racing, blood rushing to her face.

Keeping her footing here meant not mistaking the situation even slightly. Their attraction was palpable, a constant hum that vibrated between them. Something might come of that. Who knew? But there was no room for *romance*. None.

"Look," she said, popping the ring out of the box and sliding it onto her finger. "All done."

And by gosh it fitted. Like a glove. The gold was warm and smooth, the pink the perfect tone for her skin. It didn't look nearly as big and gaudy on her finger as it had in the box. It looked pretty, elegant, right.

If she'd thought her heart was racing like a rogue train before, now it was about to jump the tracks.

"Amber," said Hugo, his voice rough, as if he'd noticed it too.

So she faked a yawn. "Sorry, but I really need some sleep."

Hugo nodded, moving into the open doorway of the unfinished room next to hers.

"What time is the thing in the morning?" she asked.

Hugo looked at his watch. "We thought about two in the afternoon. Give us time for a sleep-in and time to get ready. Do you need anything until then?"

"Someone to pinch me so I know this isn't all some strange dream."

"Sorry," he said, backing away. "I've had a dose of your reality; now it's time for you to get a dose of mine."

"Quid pro quo."

He smiled. "Exactly. I'll see you in the morning?"

Which was when Amber heard the question in his voice. No wonder. The last time Hugo had planned to marry he'd been the only one to turn up.

"I'll be there," she said, and meant it.

With a nod, and a furrow of the brow, Hugo slipped into his room and quietly shut the door.

Amber did the same. She glanced over her bag, then to the bed. It had been so long since she'd slept on a mattress that hadn't been handed down a thousand times, she crawled from the end to the pillows and sank onto her back, her entire body groaning in pleasure.

She wished Ned were here now. She could do with something to cuddle. But he was in quarantine, hurrying through the requisite vet checks, and would hopefully be with them within the month.

A gentle knock rapped at her door. She sat up, heart thumping, expecting Hugo.

"Come in," she said.

Her disappointment must have been obvious as Sadie's face dropped before she glanced towards the wall connecting the two rooms.

"Sorry," said Sadie. "I know you just want some privacy and sleep. But I was upstairs feeling awful about something… There was a moment earlier when I saw you touch your tummy, and you saw me see and…"

Sadie took the few steps into the room and sat next to Amber, before taking her by the hand. When she saw the ring she stopped, a smile tugging at the corners of her mouth. "Wow. I never thought that thing could suit anybody, but you rock the rock."

Then she looked up and said, "Hugo came to visit us briefly when he was here for Reynaldo's funeral. To tell us about you. And about the baby."

Amber breathed out hard. Sadie shook Amber's hands as if hoping to shake out the sigh.

"But not to embarrass you or make you feel uncomfortable. Only so that he could insist we were gentle with you. And so that we didn't force you to stay up late and chat and tell us all about yourself, which I'd really love to do. And so I didn't try to force prawns or wine down your throat. Why prawns I have no idea. I can't remember the last time I even ate a prawn. And because he's so excited. In fact, I've never heard him talk the way he talked about you; words tripping over themselves, so many adjectives. I was actually a tad worried he'd been hypnotised until I saw you. Or, more specifically, saw him with you."

Amber had no idea what to say.

Sadie clearly took it as a sign to keep talking. "He's usually so cool. Nothing fazes him. Not even being ditched at the altar. He understood, he moved on. He can be frustratingly enlightened that way. But he followed you in here like a lost puppy. It's actually hilarious. I'm going to enjoy this very, very much."

"Well, I'm not so enlightened, just so you know. I'm rather overwhelmed right now."

"I'd be more worried if you weren't." Sadie patted her on the hand. "Just trust in Hugo, love Hugo, and you'll be right as rain."

Trust? Love? She might as well be asked to run to the moon. Amber managed to say, "Thanks for putting us up here tonight. And for organising tomorrow."

"My pleasure." With a wink Sadie was gone, leaving Amber to fall back onto the bed, splaying out like a star.

She stared at the ceiling, her mind whirling, wondering if she'd sleep at all…and was gone to the world less than three minutes later.

The next day, at just after two on a chilly winter's afternoon, with Will and Sadie as witnesses, and their office manager, Janine, throwing peony petals at their feet, Amber and Hugo were married.

CHAPTER EIGHT

"PLEASE TELL ME you are not married!"

Hugo had been reading about the measures that would be put in place to protect the royal family at the coronation, when his aunt barged into his office in the palace.

Because she'd recently lost her husband—and that barging into any room in her palace used to be within her rights—he let it go.

"I could. But that would be a lie."

"Oh, Hugo. What were you thinking?"

"Better for worse. Richer for poorer. That kind of thing."

"Hugo…"

Hugo reclined in his chair, the very picture of laid-back. "Aunt Marguerite, we didn't see the point in starting my reign with a costly wedding followed by a costly coronation, so we married atop the roof of La Tulipe with a view of the palace and friends bearing witness."

And it had been fun, of all things, everyone in a festive mood. The ceremony was a blur but afterwards they'd talked, laughed, told stories. And after the tumult of the past several months, watching that group of people get along, he felt an uncommonly large swell of pride at knowing the lot of them.

"*We?*" Marguerite looked around as if his wife might be hiding under the table.

"Her name is Amber. And you will be nice to her. Kind. Helpful. In fact, you will be her fairy godmother."

Marguerite looked as pained by the idea as he'd hoped she might. "At least tell me she can string a sentence together. That she has some semblance of class."

While he itched to tell her Amber was all that and more, Hugo folded his arms and admitted nothing. Let her sweat.

Marguerite sighed. "I had a number of lovely girls from good families lined up ready to meet you. I'd even sent out invitations for an intimate dinner party for tonight."

"Probably best you cancel."

Another sigh. "And her name is truly *Amber*?"

"Amber Giordano, Princess of Vallemont, no less." A beat, then he threw her a bone. "It was Grantley."

"I'm not sure I know the family."

Hugo laughed. "I'm sure you don't. Amber's parents are very well-respected lawyers out of Canberra." Hugo didn't know why he was building them up because Amber's background mattered not a jot to him. But it would be of interest to others. Something he hadn't considered in his hot-headed decision to throw her over his shoulder and bring her back to his cave.

"She is *Australian*?" She pressed a hand to her forehead.

"So dramatic. If you're looking to spice things up, Sadie could give you a role in one of her plays."

Marguerite lifted her head and levelled him with a look. "You look more and more like your father every year, you know. And now you have found a girl in that hot, dusty, hippy outback town and brought her here and for some reason you expect a different result."

Hugo didn't even realise he was standing until his hands hit the desk top. While it took every ounce of diplomacy he had not to erupt, his voice was like ice chips as he said, "That's enough. Amber is my wife. This time next week she will be the wife of your Sovereign Prince. And even if none of that were true, she still deserves your respect. When you meet her you will see that she is bright, articulate and lovely. She is also resolute. If you try to push her she will push back because she does not take bull from anyone. Not even me."

Marguerite kept eye contact for a long while before glancing away. "At least tell me she is beautiful."

Hugo moved around the desk and held out two hands to lift his aunt out of the chair. "Very."

"Brunette?"

"Blonde."

She winced. "At least it's better than red. Our Sadie, with that red hair of hers, would have been much harder to dress."

"I wouldn't count on it. Now go away. I am a busy man. And you have a coronation to plan."

"At least there is that." Marguerite nodded, angling her cheek for a kiss, then left.

It left Hugo feeling on edge, though quite honestly he'd been feeling on edge all day. He hadn't seen Amber since the palace chef had insisted on feeding them a private wedding banquet in the dining hall the night before. Amber had nearly fallen asleep in her dessert.

He wondered where she was right now, whether she was coping, if she was content. Though he feared he knew her well enough to know that without focus, without someone or something to look after, she would be bored out of her mind.

"Prospero?"

The big guy was through the door in a flash.

"Can you check if the package has arrived?"

Amber sat on the balcony of her rooms in the palace, huddled under a blanket, drinking ginger and honey tea to keep her nausea at bay and staring out into the very un-Australian wilderness in the distance.

To say she felt antsy would be an understatement.

While Sadie called daily and Hugo checked in as often as he could, she was used to keeping busy. Tending her bees, working at the shop, keeping Sunflower company while she painted, or taking Johnno into town to make sure he made it back again. She missed her friends. She missed Serenity. But, knowing they were only a plane flight away, mostly she missed being of use. At least Sunflower was looking after her bees.

She glanced at the side table where the pile of books Hugo had left in her room one night sat; books about princesses past. From ex-movie stars to kindergarten teachers. Women who had used their new platform to highlight children's diseases, women's rights, science, the arts, mental health.

All wrapped in an ostentatious big pink ribbon with little tiaras imprinted all over it, the gift had been given with a wink, but also a nudge. The man knew her too well.

She sat forward to read the back cover blurb when out of the corner of her eye she saw movement below…

No. It couldn't be. He wasn't due to get through quarantine for another few weeks.

But it was Ned, bounding across the grass!

Throwing off the blanket, she leaned as far over the balcony as she could without tumbling over the side to see if he had anyone with him. But he seemed to be galumphing around happily on his own. She called his name as loud as she could. But he wouldn't have heard her anyway.

So she had to go down there, find her way out of the maze of halls and staircases and wings and—

Hand to her throat, she stifled a scream. A woman cast a shadow in her doorway.

Something about her, several things in fact—the chignon, the long neck, the lean frame, the pale, elegant skirt suit, the legs locked straight on prohibitively high heels—made Amber think of her mother and she came out in an instant sweat.

Then the woman stepped out onto the balcony and Amber's panic eased.

"I startled you," said the stranger.

You think?

"I'm Princess Marguerite."

"Amber," said Amber. She held out a hand and the other woman took it, as if expecting her ring to be kissed. But Amber hadn't come this far to be kissing anyone's ring. Amber shook and let go.

"How are you settling in, my dear?"

"Gradually."

"Hmm. You're a long way from small-town Australia."

Suddenly Hugo's promise to be "on her side" had resonance. For while the Princess was being perfectly civil, Amber was fluent in the language of passive-aggressive disappointment.

Amber casually leant her backside against the brick balustrade and said, "A whole twenty-four hours by plane, in fact."

A quick smile came and went, along with a flash of surprise. "And what did you do in Serenity, Amber?"

"I was a beekeeper. And I co-ran a honey shop." She let that sit a moment before adding, "How about you, Marguerite? What do you do around here?"

The woman's eyes widened, before a smile lit her face. "My nephew warned me that if I pressed you, you would press back. I'm rather glad to see he was right."

Amber felt herself begin to relax.

"He also said you were beautiful, but he didn't tell me I had all of that to work with. The man has always underplayed his achievements."

Amber opened her mouth to protest being labelled an achievement.

But Princess Marguerite waved her hand, stopping her. "I had come in here merely to have a look at you, but now that I have I think I can skip forward a few steps and we can have an honest conversation."

"Okay."

"I stood where you are before you were even born. On the precipice of being the wife of a ruling prince." She glanced down at the pile of books on the side table next to Amber's chair and made no comment. "It's a position that requires grace, diplomacy, style, self-assurance and temerity."

Amber laughed softly. "One out of five ain't bad." Then she heard a bark and turned to look over the balcony.

Only to find Ned was not alone after all.

Hugo was there, striding across the grass in suit trousers and a dress shirt, the wind ruffling his hair and the wintry sun glinting down upon him as if he was made of gold.

He stopped, brought a hand to his mouth, and whistled loud enough for all the forest animals to hear. It worked. Ned pricked his good ear, before bounding back.

But then Hugo reached down. He threw a towel over his shoulder and picked up a bucket and a sponge. And Ned stopped so fast he practically laid down smoke.

It fast became a case of chicken. Ned, standing like a statue, waiting for Hugo to creep up on him, then bolting the moment he got close. Leaving Hugo to place hands on hips and breathe so as not to lose all patience.

Amber laughed at the ridiculousness of the sight, bringing her hands to her mouth to hold in the waves of emotion lifting and rising inside of her.

Oh, Hugo. That's not playing fair.

"What on earth is he doing?" Marguerite had joined her.

"Trying to wash my dog and failing heroically."

Amber felt Marguerite's curious gaze on her but she didn't care. No one was about to burst this bubble. Ned was here, and Hugo had made that happen. She wanted to hug them both so hard.

She cupped her hands around her mouth and called Hugo's name, but her voice didn't carry nearly far enough. So instead she held her arms tight about her and watched, smiling so hard her cheeks ached.

"Where is Prospero? Shall I summon help?"

"Nah," said Amber. "Let him figure it out himself. It's character building."

By the time Hugo managed to catch his quarry he had wet patches on his dress shirt and soap bubbles in his hair. His cheeks were pink from the cold air, and the exertion. And Ned looked so happy with all that land, the cool sunshine and the man who'd given it to him that Amber's heart clutched. Squeezing so tight she groaned.

She'd never felt anything like it in her life. As if she was filled with air and breathless all at once. It was too much. And she could no longer hold it back.

Like a stone tossed into a lake, she was falling for him. Tripping and tumbling and sinking deeper and deeper.

Not that she could ever tell him so.

She wouldn't have a clue where to start. She couldn't remember a single time her parents had told her they cared, much less used the magic word. Meaning she never had either—not once. Not even to Ned.

But mostly because the thought of putting herself out there like that terrified her to the centre of her very bones. He wouldn't laugh in her face. That wasn't Hugo's style. But what if he was ambivalent? She couldn't face that again.

No. There was no quid pro quo for this. This was a secret to keep.

She breathed out a sigh as Hugo knelt in the wet grass and Ned's muddy paws landed on his shoulders. He gave the wet dog a big rub about the ears, looking more relaxed than he had since arriving at the palace.

He was so busy, which was to be expected, but she had a new job to do too. Sure, it would be a challenge, but she thrived on challenge. And, so long as she had that man *on* her side and *at* her side, then it might well be the adventure of her life.

"Marguerite, can I ask you a favour?"

"Of course, my dear. What is it?"

"I have a pretty important event coming up and I think I might need a new dress."

"Oh, you dear girl. I thought you'd never ask."

Hugo stood behind the doors leading to the ceremonial balcony.

Marguerite had given him a kiss on the cheek before heading off to schmooze with the invited guests. His mother had even come by to wish him luck before disappearing back into the sanctuary of her rooms.

Leaving him to stare at the gap between the doors leading outside, alone.

Memories of his childhood flittered and faded; running these roads till he knew every fallen log, every hidden stream, every badger sett; slicing open a knee jumping a fence or two—he still had the scar; climbing those trees and dropping seedpods on the ancestors of the sheep that roamed there today.

Today he would officially become Sovereign Prince of all that and more. No longer merely a finance whizz, but a master of policy, of protection. Open to new ways while respecting the methods of governance and social life that had worked for generations. Beholden to the people of his country until the day he died.

He could not wait.

"Hugo?"

Hugo turned to find Amber strolling towards him. And whatever he'd been thinking about dissolved into dust motes in his mind.

For she was a vision in a sparkling pink dress that shimmered as she moved. The top hugged her curves, the skirt a feast of silk peonies swishing about her legs as she walked. A small diamond tiara nestled in her long, honey-gold hair, she looked like the Queen of the fairy folk.

Hugo swore beneath his breath. Or perhaps a little louder than that, as she shot him a quick smile.

"I know, right?" she said, giving a little twirl. "I scrubbed up well."

"Understatement of the millennium," he said, his heart thundering at the sight of her. "In fact, who cares about the coronation? I'm sure there's a broom cupboard somewhere if you'd care for a quick five minutes in heaven."

A smile quirked at the edge of her mouth and she moved closer and fussed with the brocade of his royal uniform on one shoulder. "From what I remember, you can do better than five minutes."

The world slowed to a complete stop. His wife was flirting with him.

Not that he was about to complain. In fact… He slid his hand around her waist, tugging her closer, and she let him. His voice grew low, intimate, as he said, "I wanted to thank you for my coronation gift. It was terribly thoughtful."

"What do you get for the man who has everything? I know your library is extensive, so I hoped you didn't have it."

"No. It is my very first edition of *Dog Washing for Dummies* and I will treasure it always."

She laughed then. Her soft pink mouth twisting into a smile that made his head spin.

Then the trumpets blared and the murmur of the crowd reached a crescendo. And there was no time for broom cupboards. Or flirting. Or mooning over his wife. There were more important things—

Screw it.

He pulled her in and kissed her before he could think about it. There was no hesitation; she sank into him, tipped onto her toes, her arms going around his neck as she kissed him back.

Then, far too few seconds later, she pulled back in a rush. Her gaze going to his mouth.

"Oh, no, no, no. My lipstick. You're all pink." She slid down his front, and it was all he could do not to groan. And she frantically rubbed the edge of his mouth using her thumb.

"It *is* one of our national colours. Perhaps the people might even appreciate it."

She laughed, though it was slightly hysterical.

Then the doors pressed open, letting in the wintry sunlight, the fresh Vallemontian air, and the voice and song of his people.

He let Amber go but only so far as he needed to in order to take her by the hand.

"But Marguerite said I was only to go this far."

"And do you care what Marguerite says?"

Her eyes sparked and she tucked her hand between his and looked out to the hills, tipping onto her toes to see the size of the crowd. Tens of thousands. More than the entire population of the country. She laughed. "This is insane."

"No," he said, walking her out onto the balcony, "this is us."

The coronation went without a hitch.

With the head of parliament taking Hugo's oath, tens of thousands of Vallemontian nationals as well as many tourists cheered and waved flags.

Once it was all over, Hugo and Amber retired once more to the relative quiet of the anteroom. Their gazes caught and they both burst into laughter. Then Hugo reached out to Amber, gathered her up and twirled her about, her honey-blonde waves swinging behind her.

When he put her down she smacked her fists against his chest. "Was that as much of a rush for you as it was for me? It was like a million-person love-in. They adore you, Hugo."

"Of course they do. I am adorable," he said, taking off his gloves, then undoing the buttons on his jacket and passing the accoutrements to a valet. Then, catching her eye, he said the first thing that came into his head. "I want to kiss you again very badly."

Her laughter faded, but the light remained in her eyes. "It's the dress."

"It's the woman inside the dress."

No comeback for that one.

"One of these days I'm going to crack that crotchety exterior of yours, Amber Giordano, and I'm going to find that your centre is as soft and gooey as they come."

"Dream on," she said.

"I plan on it." Then, "Do you want to get out of here?"

"More than anything."

Within half an hour they were in the palace garage.

Instructed to change into something more comfortable, Amber had taken him at his word, changing into her old jeans, boots, a jumper and a beanie.

Amber looked wide-eyed over the royal car collection; at least a small part thereof.

Hugo pointed to a small Fiat, bright yellow, laughing at how disappointed she was. "The last kind of car people would expect to see their Prince driving, so get in."

"Yes, Your Highness," she said. When she saw Ned sitting in the back seat, panting happily, she brightened. "Hey, boy. Are you coming too?"

And they were off, with Prospero and a bolstered security team discreetly on their tail.

Soon they were driving up into the foothills, heading towards the rugged landscape of Folly Cascades—the site of Vallemont's most infamous waterfall.

"This was once a primary timber area," he said, when he noticed Amber craning to see out of every window. "Prosperous from milling and hydro-power."

It was now the location of Cascade Cabins. They were small by the standards of the places he built today. Quaint and rustic, but still extremely popular. Except right now, the place was empty, the guests having been "upgraded" to the elegant Lake Glace resort over the next rise so that he would not be disturbed. So that the security team felt more comfortable too.

Hugo pulled up by a log cabin, its age evident in the ivy climbing the walls, the damp, mossy rocks lining the path and the forest that had re-grown around it.

Ned hopped out of the car first and sniffed all the lovely woodsy smells.

Amber followed close behind, rolling her shoulders, breathing deeply. "What is this place?"

"The first resort I ever built."

Her eyes swung to him. "You built this?"

His hands went into his pockets and he swung up onto his toes. "Not with my own bare hands, but yes, it was my design. My idea, my funding, my project. Validation I could be successful at something other than just a spare prince-in-waiting."

This place had been the making of him. The planning battles, the down-to-the-wire negotiations, the extreme physicality required to get a place such as this to fruition, had given him grit, built his fortitude, shown him how to deal with failure. He would be a better prince for it.

"This is what you had in mind for Serenity?"

Hugo's gaze swung back to Amber. "My style has evolved since I built this place, as well as my budget. But I imagine a similar kind of 'grown out of the environment' feeling to the place. This, but with every modern luxury."

She breathed out hard through her nose, then looked with a fresh eye, taking in lush surroundings, the quiet overlaid with sounds of birdsong, of forest animals, the comfortably rustic aesthetic.

Hugo knew the moment she found the sign. A

couple of days back he'd had it made, the words
"The Shack" burned into a piece of wood. It was
now attached to the front door of the small cabin
ahead.

She walked slowly up onto the porch, barely
noticing when Ned ran past chasing a butterfly.

Hugo followed. "If you ever need a time-out,
a break from the crazy goings-on of the palace,
this cabin can be your escape. There's a spare
room, which I thought we could set up as a nursery. Perhaps get a fold-out couch in case of visitors. But I'll leave all that up to you, since it is
your coronation gift."

"My...? But I gave you a book."

"Which I will read from cover to cover. Now
back to my gift. I asked Maintenance to take the
door off its hinges, and to put a hammer to a couple of the walls to make it feel more like home,
but—"

"Shut up," she said, her voice ragged. "Just shut
up."

And then she threw herself at him. Literally.
Her feet left the ground and he wrapped her up
tight, right as her lips found his.

The soft, sweet taste of her was like an elixir,
scrambling his thoughts. But not so much that he
couldn't find the door. He yanked it open, carrying her inside using one arm.

He kicked the front door closed—his security

team was out there somewhere and there they could stay—and together they stumbled into the main room, where a fire crackled in the hearth.

They backed into the room, narrowly missing couches and end tables, and bumping into a lamp that threatened to topple. Then Amber's toes caught on the floor or the rug, acting as a brake, and Hugo twisted to take the brunt of the fall. He rolled so that she was beneath him, her hair splayed out across the fur.

Her chest rose to meet his as she breathed heavily, her dark eyes looked unblinking into his. He lowered his face, achingly slowly, and brushed his lips across hers.

Then suddenly she scrunched her eyes shut tight. "This is too much."

For Hugo it wasn't nearly enough.

"I can't take all this…this romance."

"Is that what this is?"

"Come on, Hugo. The cars, the sign, the fireplace. You're romancing me." She stuck her left hand in his face, showing off the ring. "At this point in time, it's pretty much moot."

Hugo took her hand, kissed her knuckles and then turned her hand over and kissed her palm. "I beg to differ. We did this all backwards, you see."

She blinked. He kissed the tips of her fingers one by one.

"We fell into bed together. And then we fell out.

Then we fell pregnant. And then we eloped. We missed this part, you see. The drives, the dates, the romance."

She breathed and said nothing.

"Now, will you shut up and let me woo my wife?"

He let her hand drop back to her chest and looked into her eyes, where he saw hope, timid and shy; emotion, ragged and true; desire and slow sexual unfurling.

"No more talk," she said, her voice barely a whisper. "I've had enough talk. From Sadie and Marguerite. From the protocol people and the ladies-in-waiting. Even Prospero has found his voice. Did you know he has a thing for insects? I've never answered so many questions about bees as I have this week."

"No more talk," Hugo promised.

"I'm a girl of action."

"Then let's get you some." Hugo ran a hand down her side, holding himself together by the skin of his teeth as her body undulated beneath his touch.

"More," she said, and he wondered how he had gone this long without touching her, tasting her, revelling in her beautiful abandon.

He kissed the bottom of her jaw and the soft spot below her ear.

He knew her tells—like the way she nibbled

at her bottom lip. But there was something new here too. A new tension that had her in its grip.

"It's okay if you're nervous."

She flung her eyes open. "I'm not nervous."

"I'd understand," he said, taking advantage of her open mouth and tugging on her lower lip until her eyes near rolled back in her head. Then, "The last time we did this, I was merely a man. This time you'll be making love to a prince."

It took a moment for her to come back to him, but when she did she burst into laughter. "If you believe it makes a difference, prove it."

"As you wish," Hugo murmured, and set about doing just that.

It was agony taking it slow. The sweetest agony there was. But he took his time undressing her, caressing her, stretching out her pleasure. Until her breaths grew ragged, her hands clung to him and she rolled and writhed beneath the touch of his fingers, his mouth.

When he kissed her belly he did so with all the gentleness he could manage. He kissed to the right of her belly button, then the left, breathing in the scent of her skin, letting the knowledge that a part of him grew inside of her wash over him.

He rose to kiss her. She lifted to catch the kiss.

When he pulled back her eyes caught on his— dark, sensual, nearly lost to pleasure.

He stopped torturing her—torturing himself—

and joined her. Neither looked away as they rocked together. As they made love.

Then Amber gasped, gripping him, her fingers digging into his arms. Heat and pleasure and emotion collected inside his core, before flooding through him like a lava flow.

While a single tear travelled down the edge of her cheek, manifesting the stunning emotion welling behind her eyes. No hiding. No pretending. No secrets. As if he could see all the way to her soul.

It was sumptuous. It was undefended.

It was his.

"What does *miele* mean?" she asked, her voice sleepy.

"Hmmm?"

"You call me that sometimes."

Did he? He hadn't noticed. But then, it did suit her. "It means honey."

Amber smiled up at him before rolling onto her side and taking his arm to place it over her like a cage. She snuggled into the cradle of his body. Within moments her breathing slowed.

While Amber drifted gently to sleep, Hugo had never felt so awake in his entire life.

An hour later, Hugo stood by the window, looking unseeingly into the forest beyond, his mind still freewheeling.

He was married to the most compelling woman he had ever known. They had a child on the way, and he had just been crowned Sovereign Prince of the country he loved.

It was a strange and unexpectedly difficult moment to realise he had everything he could ever want.

Philosophically, he knew that he should be crowing. Instead he felt as if he was careening towards the edge of a cliff.

He glanced back at Amber, who lay asleep on the fluffy rug by the fire, curled up in a ball beneath the throw he'd laid over her, not quite covering her dandelion tattoo. Her face was gentled in sleep.

As if the things he had to face—the security threats, the debilitating weight of overwhelming bureaucracy that remained after such a long reign—had nothing to do with her. But they did, as she was his wife. Making it far harder to make clear decisions when how it would affect her was never far from his mind.

He could no longer pretend that this was a mere marriage of convenience; a prince in need of a princess, a child in need of a father. There were feelings here—deep, broad, twisty, ingrained, developing, reaching feelings.

It would not have concerned him nearly as much if it had been one-sided. He had been stuck on Amber from the moment they had met.

But now he was certain Amber felt something for him too. He'd seen it in her eyes. Felt it in her touch. He'd tasted it as he'd kissed away the tear as she'd fallen asleep in his arms.

He could not offer any more than he already had—a beautiful home, the opportunity to do real good in the world, and as much help raising their child as she desired. But truly tender feelings? Love?

At thirty-two years of age his growing was all done. His heart was as big as it was ever going to get.

And yet making love to Amber, as her husband, had created a shift inside of him, allowing an aching kind of regret to bleed through the cracks. Only proving that, while he would not bend, he could still break.

As Sovereign Prince of the great nation of Vallemont, breaking was not an option. He would not make the mistakes his father had made and screw it all up.

He crouched down, pressing her hair away from her face, and forced himself to ignore the heat rushing through him. "Amber. *Miele*, wake up."

One eye opened, and then the other. Her hair was all messed up, her face pink with sleep, leaving him feeling disorientated with desire.

You can do this. You can resist. It's the only way.

"Did I snore?" she asked. "I dreamt I was snoring."

"Like an ogre," he lied.

She breathed sleepily. Then she ruffled her hair and yawned and Hugo felt such a heady mix of affection and bone-deep attraction it threatened to take his legs out from under him.

It seemed that decades of protocol would no longer be enough. He would have to keep his wife at arm's length in order not to slip again. It might well be the hardest thing he ever had to do, but it was the price he had to pay to take on the role for which he had prepared for his entire life.

"I just had the best dream," she said, her words sliding into a yawn. "The best part? Waking up and knowing real life was better."

Then she reached up to touch his face. Wound so tightly, he couldn't help but flinch, his entire body physically recoiling from her touch.

Amber saw it too. She suddenly went stiff, as if the blood had drained out of her extremities. "Hugo?"

He squared his shoulders and stood. "It's time to go."

"Already?"

"I'm needed back at the palace."

"Shortest honeymoon ever." She tried for a joke, her brow furrowing when he didn't smile.

"But I guess the beauty of being married to the owner means we can come back any time."

It was. But it could never happen. Not if he had any chance of being the kind of prince he'd always wanted to be.

"Come on." He held out a hand. Hesitating, she took it, allowing him to help her to her feet.

Confusion flashed behind her eyes, as well it might. She searched his face for the reason for his reticence.

The urge to explain was near overwhelming. But confessing his feelings would only put the onus on her, which was entirely unfair.

In that moment, he found himself understanding his forebears. Keeping separate apartments wasn't a simple matter of conflicting social hours, or full closets, or accommodating separate staff; it was a necessary form of self-protection.

Then Amber straightened her shoulders, pulled the blanket around her and said, "Okay, then. I guess that's that. I'll collect my things."

He made to let her go, but then at the last— blaming the streak of self-destruction he could have inherited from either of his parents—he took her by the hand and twirled her into his arms and placed a gentle kiss on her lips.

She sank into him without hesitation, his beautiful, fierce, impossible Princess.

When she pulled back she looked into his eyes

for a moment. And this time she pressed away. As if she was so used to being dismissed that closing herself off was the easier path for her too.

It was why he was sure this could work.

The both of them were so screwed up they would never let love get in the way of a good thing.

CHAPTER NINE

THE MORNING AFTER the coronation, Amber lay on the colossal bed in her private apartment feeling nothing.

Not sick. Not any more. The usual gnawing sensation had gone from her belly. She was simply… blank.

She stared at the canopy over her bed, her gaze skimming brocade and fringing, lace and…were those crystals? The workmanship was beautiful. Exquisite even. Sunflower would take one look at the detail and burst into happy tars.

But Amber couldn't seem to find the energy to care.

Perhaps it was because she'd grown up with money—with prestige, luxury, really nice bedding—and had turned her back on it.

That was the thing her friends had been so shocked about. Not the fact she felt misunderstood and overlooked to the point of legally emancipating herself, but that it had been enough for her to turn her back on the rewards.

Over the first few years she'd questioned her decision more than once—when she'd been hungry, broke, when she'd had every one of her meagre possessions stolen from a cheap motel.

Until she'd followed the Southern Cross and arrived in Serenity.

From the moment she'd looked up that hill, over that field of lavender, she'd felt vindicated in her choice to follow her own path. For she had found people who opened their arms to anyone. Heck, Hugo had planned to rearrange their entire existence and they'd welcomed him in and said, "Let's see what you have to say." Every decision they made came from a place of acceptance. Of love.

People were life's true reward. Having a community to rely on. Having a community rely on her.

She'd met Hugo while high on their goodness, in a single glance seeing him as worthy of her time, and over time finding him a man of honour and depth, of humour and heat. A man who truly seemed to value her, not for what she could do for him but because of the qualities he saw in her. The elusive something she'd been searching for her entire life.

It was their fault that she'd believed his promises.

Waking in front of the fire on their "honeymoon", she'd felt so happy. That a man as busy as he, with all the pressures he was under, had taken the time to create something private, something uniquely them. It had been a few seconds of pure and utter bliss.

And then she had opened her eyes.

There had been nothing in particular that she could put her finger on. Only that he'd seemed cool, detached; like a marble bust of a prince rather than flesh and blood.

On the drive back to the palace he'd asked her questions, answered hers; his hands had been relaxed on the wheel. But nothing was as it had seemed before. Nothing at all. Suddenly, the wintry cold outside was nothing compared to the chill within.

Which was when she'd realised it had all been in her head.

That she was so desperate for affection she'd believed the fairy tale. But it had been nothing but an illusion created by a broken, lonely girl.

Finding some deep reserve of energy, she pulled herself to sitting then padded over to the dressing table and sat.

The reflection in the mirror was of a woman she barely knew. Her hair was a mess, her eyes dark and sleepy; her cheeks a little leaner than usual, a result of barely keeping her food down for days. But that would change. She'd fill out, become smooth and rosy and plump.

The baby that had connected them in some quiet, magical way suddenly felt vulnerable. As if she hadn't been as diligent in her protection as she'd promised.

Amber put a hand over her belly and said, "Shh. It's all right. It's all going to be okay."

And then a knock came at the door.

Marguerite didn't wait for a response before entering. A plethora of strangers followed in her wake.

Amber grabbed the fine mohair throw from the back of the chair and wrapped it around her shoulders to cover her thin T-shirt and bare legs.

"Good morning, Your Highness."

"Good morning." She ran a quick hand over her bed hair and edged over to the Princess. "Marguerite? Who are these people?"

"My dear, I'd like to introduce you to your staff." One by one Marguerite pointed to the people in the line, listing hairdresser, make-up artist, stylist, linguists, personal planner, personal cook, and other positions she didn't quite catch.

She gave a double-take to the cook, who had the same wild strawberry-blonde waves as Sunflower, but the woman's smile was tight. Not like sunny Sunflower's at all.

So this was her new "community": a group of strangers whose job it was to tell her what to do, how to look, talk and dress, what to eat and where to go.

It didn't feel right. Not a bit. In fact, it felt horribly familiar.

She glanced towards the door, but what was she

going to do? Complain to Hugo? He was so busy. And after the day before, she was no longer sure how firmly on her side he really was.

Instead, she turned to Marguerite, who looked positively buoyant as she pressed one last woman forward. In her fifties, with a tight grey bun and a stern countenance, she looked like the nasty principal from a Roald Dahl novel.

"Hi," said Amber as the woman loomed over her. "And you are...?"

"This," said Marguerite, "is Madame Brassard. She is the nanny."

Amber stilled. It took everything in Amber not to put a hand to her belly. "The what, now?"

"The nanny. For when the time comes, in the future, that you and Hugo are blessed with children, Madame Brassard will be assisting you in their day-to-day care. She has impeccable credentials, has worked with several important families, although non-disclosure agreements mean I cannot say who."

Having a breakdown was bad enough. Having one in front of a room full of strangers, some of whom probably didn't even understand a word she was saying, was a mortifying thought.

"Marguerite, may I please talk to you in private?"

"Dear girl, I'm afraid that the moment you become a Giordano there is no such thing as private any more. Especially from these good people."

"But I don't know these people."

"You will. In good time. They are your team, my dear."

Ah, no, she would not. Amber's hackles were now screaming.

"I actually prefer to build my own teams, if it's all right with you."

"Unfortunately, that is not possible. We have security to consider. Tradition. Royal protocol."

With every one of Marguerite's attempts to block her, Amber felt the walls closing in. She held up both hands in the international sign for stop. "I don't give a flying hoot about royal protocol. I truly don't."

Marguerite's eye twitched. "You married a prince, my dear. And not just any prince. The Sovereign Prince. It comes with responsibilities…"

Amber held up a finger to hush her, and the "team" all gasped in shock. But Amber's head was now buzzing so hard it might as well have been filled with bees. "Semantics aside, I did not marry a prince. I married a man. I married Hugo. A man who I may, one day, have children with. And if I do, it was made very clear that I will raise them myself." She added a belated, "With him."

Marguerite's expression was unreadable, though

Amber could have sworn she saw a flicker of respect.

"Where's Hugo? I need Hugo."

Marguerite snapped her fingers, the lady-in-waiting leaping to her side. "Sofia, send word to the Prince that—"

"Wait! No. Thank you, Sofia, but you do not have to send word. I'm a smart woman with two feet and the ability to put one in front of the other. I can find the Prince myself."

With that she left her parody of a "commune" in her rooms. She tracked down Hugo in his apartment, which was down the hall and around a couple of bends. Seriously, who lived that way and called it a relationship? It was insane.

This whole thing was insane.

Her head spinning, her heart racing, she came to a halt in the open doorway when she saw Hugo was with his "team" too.

Prospero noticed her in an instant. "Your Highness?"

"Just a moment," said Hugo, sitting on the banquette at the end of his big bed, paper resting on his knee. Her heart squeezed at the sight of him, turning her into a mess of confusion and need.

"Hugo," Prospero said, his voice more insistent than Amber had ever heard it.

Hugo clearly felt the same way, as his gaze swung past his muscle man to Amber. Whatever he saw on her face brought him to his feet, eating up the floor and coming to her side.

"*Miele*, what is wrong? What happened? Is it—?"

His hands reached out to hold her before they stopped mid-air, as if a remote control had changed him from go to stop. The anxiety ramped from an eight to an eleven.

Then he stared at her belly as if an alien were about to explode out of her.

"No." She looked around at the half-dozen others in the room, each one looking out of the window or at their feet. "It's not that."

He breathed out hard. "Good. Excellent."

And then he took a step back and put his hands into his pockets, the disconnection as strong as if he had shut the door in her face.

And whatever anxiety she had felt at Marguerite's intrusion was nothing on the emotional wreck she became in that moment.

She somehow found words, saying, "I can see you are busy, but do you have a moment?"

He breathed out hard, and looked around at the dozen people all vying for his attention. He ran a hand through his hair and it stayed messy. He looked beleaguered. And it made her heart twist, just a smidge, to note that he was struggling too.

"Just one minute," she said, holding onto the very last hope that she was reading things wrong;

giving him a chance to show her that she was wrong. That he *was* on her side. That he did care. That she could count on him as she'd thought.

Then he said, "Give me five minutes to finish up here and I'll come find you."

He hovered a hand near her back, ostensibly shooing her from the room. Once she was over the threshold he nodded at one of his lackeys, who closed the door in her face.

And something inside of her came away. Like a rowing boat snapping its moorings and drifting out to sea.

On numb feet she headed back to her room. Aware that, when it came down to it, it wasn't even really his fault. She'd never asked for affection. In fact, she'd made it clear she didn't want any of that kind of guff.

He'd given it anyway. And now she was used to it. To how it felt to be a part of something real, something warm. A community of two.

And she would never accept anything less than that again.

It was more like an hour before Hugo was finally able to drag himself away.

Unable to come up with a reason not to, he'd been forced to fire half the people on the board of the transport department for bad management bordering on state fraud. When he'd agreed to take on the position he'd never imagined his first week would be so onerous.

But it was compensated for by the security breakthrough. Prospero's compatriots had tracked down and rounded up the misanthropes who had orchestrated the attack on his uncle at the picnic all those months ago. The same ones who'd been causing strong headaches for Security since Hugo's return, a burr that had lived in the back of his head. And they were singing like canaries.

Still, starved and emotionally raw, his whole body felt like one big ache.

But he'd promised Amber some time. And the truth was, he could do with seeing her. Despite his best efforts at keeping his distance, for both their sakes, it turned out he couldn't function—not in the capacity he desired—without her keeping his head on straight.

His feet no longer dragged as he strode down the hall towards Amber's apartment.

"Amber?" he called from the open doorway.

No response.

He poked his head into her room to find it empty when he'd expected laughter and noise. And arguments, to be sure. For Marguerite had volunteered to get Amber acquainted with people who could guide her in the coming months. And, hoping to keep his aunt distracted from her woe, he'd agreed.

Where was everyone?

Where was Amber?

With security on his mind, he didn't like this one bit. "Amber?" he called more loudly this time, his ear straining, his heart thunderous.

"In here."

The sound of her voice, coming from her dressing room, brought a rush of relief.

But he pulled up short when he found her. She'd changed into warm clothes—boots, jeans, an oversized jumper that kept falling off one shoulder, and her hair fell in golden waves from beneath a beanie the colour of lavender that Sunflower had knitted for her before they'd left.

And she was folding clothes into a suitcase.

Ned sat at her feet, looking the way dogs looked when they thought they were in trouble. Only Hugo knew Ned wasn't the one Amber was mad at.

"Amber?"

She looked up. She seemed tired, fragile. He ached just looking at her.

"Amber, what's going on?"

"You said I could leave at any time."

The word *no* almost tore from deep inside, but he held it at bay. Just. He moved deeper into the room and said, "And I meant it."

He told his hands to go into his pockets so that he would not touch her, but one moved to her elbow, gently stopping her from packing. He turned her to face him, and she didn't even try to stop him. As if she was hollow. As if she had no fight left to give.

He placed a finger beneath her chin, lifting until he could see her face. As beautiful as the first time he'd seen her. More so now that he knew the mind that whirled behind it, the vast heart that held her together.

"Talk to me," he said, his voice raw.

She closed her eyes for a second before they fluttered open, hitting him with all that whisky-brown delight. "Do you need me here, Hugo?"

Hugo baulked. It wasn't what he'd been expecting. Or a side of her he'd ever seen before. She sounded almost brittle. It rang of Marguerite.

"Amber, please—"

"No. After meeting the vast number of people I apparently need to make me a palatable princess, I'm pretty sure I'll be nothing but a distraction." She threw a shirt into her bag. Then another. "A hindrance to your ability to do what you have to do. Especially in these early days of transitioning."

It was so close to what he'd been thinking the day before that he baulked again. Only she made it sound as if she was a burden when the truth was the polar opposite. "Amber, stop bloody packing, will you? I want you here. I would not have asked it of you unless I believed it was the right decision. If I didn't know that my country would benefit from your…" Heart, soul, fierce upstanding goodness.

She stopped, some item of clothing scrunched in her hand. "My what?"

"Your innate knack for ferreting out trouble."

Coward, his subconscious muttered.

No, he shot back. *The smart move.*

Because he knew what she wanted to know. He could see it in the set of her shoulders; hear it in the raw scrape of her voice. She wanted to know how he truly felt about her.

But he couldn't tell her what she wanted to hear. For, while he wanted her, while he cared for her so deeply it was disorienting, he didn't *need* anyone. He'd amputated that part of himself when he was a younger man.

And yet, with Amber, he wasn't even half as afraid of losing her as he was of loving her.

Which was how he managed to say, "I am married. I am of age. I am crowned. I needed you to ensure all that was possible. And for which I will be eternally grateful. But hereon in, whatever you decide to do will not affect that."

She blinked at him then, like a puppy who'd been kicked out of the house during a downpour. Marguerite had earned a reprieve. Now he wanted to throttle himself instead.

Amber grabbed a pile of clothes and threw them into the case without folding them, then she slammed the case shut, zipping with all her might. "That's just great. I hope you know how lucky you are, going through life so blithely unaffected. I hope the people of Vallemont know what a big-hearted leader they have."

She grabbed the bag, and hauled it past him into her bedroom.

"And where exactly are you planning to go?"

"I'm not sure."

"You can't just walk out the front door."

"You think so?" She turned on him then. She had her fight back—thank goodness—her spirit so strong it burned in her eyes. "Watch me."

Screw it, he thought. Screw holding back. Screw the job. Screw everything but this woman. He took the three steps to meet her and hauled her into his arms and kissed her.

She resisted for a fraction of a second, anger and hurt still raging inside her. Before tossing her suitcase to the floor and wrapping her arms about him and kissing him with such unbridled passion it took his breath away.

It felt like days since he'd touched her, not hours. All the energy spent thinking about keeping her at arm's length only making the abandon more intense.

She tasted like honey and sunshine and everything good as she sank into him, and he into her. Basking, exploring, until the world contracted to the size of her.

He might not need her, not in the way she needed him to, but God how he wanted her. In his arms, in his bed, in his life.

He spread his hands over her back, sliding his thumbs up her sides, catching her sweater until he reached skin. Silken soft, hot from the inside.

She gasped, her head falling away, leaving him scope to trail kisses along her jaw, down her neck. As her body melted against him, he feared he might tell her whatever the hell she wanted to hear. So he wrapped his arms more tightly around her; holding on for dear life.

When the backs of her knees pressed into the bed, he lowered her down and they fell together. Landing in a mass of twisted limbs. Their ragged breaths snagged against the silence.

And Amber looked into his eyes, deep, searching. Her hair splayed out around her like waves of sunlight, her lips pink from kissing.

Hugo ran his thumb down her cheek and she turned her cheek to rub into his touch.

Then she lifted a hand as if about to run it through his hair…

Only at the last she stopped, pressing against his chest with her other hand to push him away and disentangling her legs so fast she nearly fell off the bed.

And she split the heavy silence with a growl. That turned into a roar. That had even near-deaf Ned jogging out of the dressing room to make sure she was all right.

"I can't do this! I won't. I spent my entire childhood collecting the rare drops of attention from my parents and waiting in agony for the next. Do you know why I divorced them? Really why?"

Hugo hooked his feet over the edge of the bed and ran a hand down his face. Still trying to collect his wits, he shook his head.

"That paperwork was physical proof that my life was mine. No one else's. That it would, from that moment on, be lived on my terms. Those terms were hard for a really long time. Scary at times. But I got through it, because I knew that, no matter what, my choices were mine. I won't do hot and cold, Hugo. Not now. Not ever."

Hugo had never felt more like a grown-up than he did in that moment. And it wasn't as much fun as the brochures had made out. "Are you saying you want a divorce?"

"What? No. I don't think so." A beat went by then she shook her head. "We had a contract and I plan to honour that contract. But I need some time away to come to terms with what we are. What we *really* are. I think I've been stuck on those two lonely people who shared a small, lumpy bed and talked in ridiculous streams of consciousness until three in the morning. But that was the fairy tale."

Finally her hands went to her belly. "We have a baby coming, Hugo, and that's as real as it gets. To be ready for that I need to shake this off. This feeling…" She glanced at him—a flash of hurt, a flash of heat—and something squeezed deep inside his chest.

"How much time?"

"As much as it takes."

Hugo ran a hand over his face. To think he knew a dozen perfectly lovely women who would have fallen over themselves to be Princess. Women who could have led a civil, courteous, undramatic life by his side. And he'd have been bored out of his mind.

Amber had never been the safe choice, or even the smart choice, but she had been his only choice. Choice being the important word. For the choice was also hers. To stay or to go.

For all his faults, he was no bastard. He wouldn't keep her if she wanted to go. Even with the possible future of his country growing inside of her. But once he had a handle on this behemoth job of his, he'd track her down wherever in the world she landed and bring her home.

"All right," he said. His mind was set, but his

voice was raw. "On the proviso you allow me to assign security."

Her expression grew thunderous. "Hugo—"

"That's non-negotiable. I know you, Amber. I know you'd take on a dragon if it looked sideways at someone you cared about. I need to know that you are safe."

She swallowed, her eyes giving nothing away. Then she nodded.

"You must also promise you'll find appropriate housing—heated, with walls that actually keep out the wind."

At mention of the shack her expression softened. "No buckets to catch the drips?"

"Stairs that don't crack when you walk on them. Railings that don't wobble. Working plumbing."

She glanced towards the bathroom with its double shower and claw-footed bathtub. "I do like working plumbing."

His voice was rough as he said, "You will have a bank account at your disposal. And access to the best doctors. For the baby."

"Thank you. Any other demands, Your Highness?"

The only words that made their way out of his mouth were, "Come back soon."

Then, aware of how close he'd come to completely giving himself away, he added, "You can do good here, Amber. So much good. I hope, in time, you find that level of service reward enough."

She swallowed. Nodded. And picked up her suitcase.

Even while Hugo's head hurt with the effort not to command her to stay, he did as so many princes had done before him and leant on history, on convention, on duty and said, "So be it."

He moved to the side of the bed and pressed a button in the panel. A knock came at the door moments later. "Come in."

Prospero entered.

"Prospero, could you please organise a car for Amber?"

The big man glanced at Amber, then Hugo, at Amber's suitcase, concern lighting his stern, solid features. "Where shall I say the car is to take her?"

"The airport. From there the family plane will take her wherever she wishes to go."

"If that is her wish."

"It is," Amber said. "I'll call. Let you know when I'm settled. Don't worry about me. I'll be fine."

Hugo wasn't worried about her. He was worried about himself.

But it was too late to do anything about it as she gave Hugo one last long look, then walked out of the bedroom door. Gone. For how long, he did not know. Where to? He did not know that either. He couldn't remember ever feeling this ineffective.

"Your Highness." Prospero's voice was tight.

Hugo held up a hand—he didn't want to hear it. When he saw his hand was shaking he shoved it into a pocket.

"Your Highness," Prospero insisted. Then, breaking protocol for the first time since they'd known one another, said, "What the hell happened?"

"Stay with her. Keep her safe. She's…" *Important*, he'd been about to say, but it felt so cold compared with how much she meant to him. "She's wily. Even more so than I was."

"I will protect her as if she's my own." Prospero nodded and then was gone, leaving Hugo feeling more alone than he remembered feeling his entire life.

As if sensing his loss, Ned padded over to Hugo and sat on his foot, looking up at him with his strange mismatched eyes. Hugo sank his hand into the dog's soft fur. "I know, buddy. But this is life. People come, people go. And some make such an impact they leave a crater that never quite heals."

Hugo gave Ned one last rub before the dog harrumphed and left to follow his girl out of the door. Then he looked around Amber's apartment, the unmade bed, the open door to the wardrobe she'd never had the chance to fill.

Everyone he cared for left. Died. Ran. Or slowly slipped away.

But now was not the time to be morose. It was time to focus. He would be the best damn prince they had ever seen.

All he'd ever wanted, deep down, was to follow the family tradition, to be a true Giordano.

Now he was prince of all he surveyed. Even as his private life lay in tatters.

"Well, what do you know?" he said out loud. "You're a Giordano, through and through."

CHAPTER TEN

"TOLD YOU WE'D find him here. What is he wearing? Is he drunk? Give him the coffee."

Hugo had smelled the warm, hazy scent before he heard Sadie's voice. He opened one eye just enough to see Will shrug. Good man.

"I don't think I've ever actually seen him drunk. Is he allowed to get drunk, being the leader of the country? What if he has to decide on the blue wire or the red wire and he's too drunk to remember which is which?"

Will gave Sadie a look. "I'm not sure nuclear launch codes are something you need to be concerned about in Vallemont."

"True. I'm just worried. I've never seen him like this."

Will pressed forward, his face darkening. "I have. The last two times his world fell apart. Mate!" he said, giving Hugo a shake.

"I'm awake." Awake enough to feel the press of a rogue stone from the wall of the tallest turret in the castle wall pressing into his back. "And I'm not drunk. I'm merely exhausted."

For he had barely slept a night since Amber had walked out of his door.

He'd worked. And worked. And worked. Wrangling with parliament. Sweeping through government departments, cleaning house like an avenging angel. And dealing with the reason behind the security threat that had dogged his family for months.

When there was no other work to be done he'd spent his time in the garden. Washing Ned—for all its challenges—had been therapeutic. On a whim, he'd had his staff install a kind of modified greenhouse. And he worked in it daily. It was so physically demanding it was the only thing that could send him into a dead sleep when he needed it most.

In fact, he'd been working in there before he'd followed his feet and ended up here.

The staff called it his Zen Garden. He wondered if it might yet kill him.

Will added, "Then stop eavesdropping and get the hell up. You're worrying my woman."

Hugo gave Sadie a look, realised she was truly worried, then pulled himself to standing.

He held out his hand for the mug and Will handed it over. Sadie moved to stand beside him, crossing her arms but near enough to nudge with her elbow. She gave him a once-over, her gaze stopping a moment on his torn jeans, battered sneakers, holey beanie. "This is a new look for you."

"I've been gardening."

"You what, now?"

Hugo took a long sip, closing his eyes against the bliss of the bitter taste. Strong, black. Laced with something medicinal. No wonder Will was his oldest friend.

Thankfully Sadie changed the subject, though it wasn't any easier. "How is Amber?"

"Safe," he said, which was the most important thing.

"Have you heard from her?"

"Prospero has been sending updates."

Hourly at times, good man.

Amber wasn't sleeping well. The nausea seemed to have abated. She looked pale. She laughed at a joke. She was reading children's books, making lists. Baking. She wasn't good at it and he hoped she'd give it up.

"Is she okay?"

He sipped on his coffee again.

"Jeez," Sadie muttered, "it's like pulling teeth."

"If you are looking for news I can update you on the security issue."

"Fine. Do that."

"The group who attacked Reynaldo all those months ago was led by the husband of a woman Reynaldo had…befriended. The husband had found out, fallen into the waiting arms of a cuckolded husbands help group, and in a frenzy of misguided support together they made the bungled attack."

Sadie blinked. "For *that* I nearly married you? I could kill Reynaldo right now. You know, if he was still alive." Then her eyes narrowed. "So what does this have to do with Amber?"

His clever friend knew him all too well. "There has been chatter since I arrived back home that something else was in the planning. The leader, the man who'd lost his wife, got it into his head that—considering my father's infamous infidelity and now my uncle's—I would be next to have a go at his wife. So they were planning to have a go at mine."

Neither Sadie nor Will laughed.

"Oh, Hugo. You must have been terrified."

Terrified didn't even come close. The shake in Hugo's hand still came over him every now and then when he thought about it.

"The leader now realises how twisted his thinking had become and is all remorse and apology. It's over. Happy ending all round."

Sadie looked to Will and mouthed something Hugo didn't catch.

"I saw that," said Hugo.

"What?"

He put down the coffee, cleared his throat, ran hard hands through his hair and looked at Sadie. This place, this turret, had been their favourite spot as kids. The place they'd run to when feeling hard done by, or in need of some peace and quiet; to sort out their heads.

In the days since Amber had left he'd wanted to move into the turret. Maybe for ever.

"If it's such a happy ending, why are you hiding on our turret?"

Good question.

"Only one way to turn that frown upside down. Go get your girl."

"She's in Serenity." Probably. "Surrounded by lavender fields and stingless honey bees, where she belongs. And if Serenity makes her happy then I'm not about to take it away from her."

"Right. Because you're in love with her."

Hugo kept his trap shut. The strength of his feelings for his wife did not matter—how he acted on them did. That was the lesson to be learned from all this.

The problems his uncle had left behind were due to him making the easy choices over the right ones, leading to blackmail, extortion and leaving behind his wife and young family. Hugo planned to fix it all.

"Don't panic. It's quite normal to be in love with your wife. Right, Will?" Sadie asked.

"So I hear."

"What are you talking about?" Hugo asked.

"What are *you* talking about?" she shot back.

"How I can best serve Vallemont, redeem the family name and sleep at night."

"By being a loving husband and father first, of course."

"Leo, for Pete's sake. Leave it the hell alone."

"Fine!" She threw her hands in the air and paced to the other side of the turret. "But just one last thing. She knows how you feel, right? Before she left you told her you loved her and that's why you had to let her go?"

Hugo turned and gripped the rock wall, looked over verdant farmland, craggy mountains, the road he and Amber had travelled from the airport. And he said, "Not in so many words."

"Okay, but you told her when you proposed to her."

Hugo kept his mouth shut again.

"How did you propose, Hugo? We never heard the story. Knowing how you proposed to me, I'm assuming you learnt your lesson and did it right this time."

Hugo thought back to the words he had used. The offer he had made. He tried to pretty it up but in the end simply said, "I made it impossible for her to refuse."

Sadie's face sank into her hand, her laughter rueful. "Hugo, Hugo, Hugo!"

"She prides herself on being pragmatic."

"Then that's why she agreed to marry you. But did you tell her why you wanted to marry *her*?"

"I don't understand."

"Of course you don't. And maybe I wouldn't have either before I met Will. Hugo, you're *in love with her*."

"Yes, all right, I'm in love with her. I've been in love with her since I first laid eyes on her, looking down at me with those wild whisky eyes, telling me off for invading her hammock, all the while looking at me like I'm a hot lunch." Hugo pressed away from the wall and paced about the turret. "I've never met anyone who makes me feel like I'm floating an inch above the ground while also so grounded in my own reality I can see it, smell it, taste it fully for the first time in my life. Who makes me feel…" He thumped a fist against his chest. "She makes me feel. And not having her near, not knowing when I'll see her again… I can't sleep. I can't function. I'm running on automatic."

Sadie sighed. "Was that so hard?"

"That was more difficult than you can possibly imagine!"

She gave his arm a squeeze. "And it didn't occur to you to lead with all that, when you asked her to be yours?"

"She prides herself—"

"On being pragmatic. Yes, so you said. So do we all, unless we are given reason to believe in the alternative. She might *want* to be pragmatic, Hugo. But what she needs, what all of us need, is affection, consideration, love. Some of us also need a rockin' hot prince. Or a puppy. Will, can we get a puppy?"

"We live in a construction zone, so no."

"Okay."

Hugo only heard the last of it in his periphery, for he was onto something. His brain having switched from automatic to clear and present. "A phone. I need a phone."

Sadie looked to Will, who was way ahead of her. He handed it over then took Sadie by the wrist, drawing her away, murmuring to her about giving him space.

Hugo called Prospero. The big guy answered on the third ring. Didn't wait for a hello before asking, "Where is Ned?"

A beat, then, "Your Highness?"

"If she went back to Serenity, Ned would be in quarantine. She would never have put him through that twice in such a short space of time. So where is she?"

But Hugo knew before he'd even finished the question.

"If you tell me she's been staying in the shack just up the road all this time, while I've been out of my mind worried about her, trying to run the country without her, I will send you on a mission to Siberia."

"Then I won't tell you that."

Hugo tried.

"I do like what you've done with the garden, Your Highness. Very Zen."

Hugo hung up, paced towards the exit, then turned to give Will back his phone. Then he was off, running down the winding staircase before he even had any semblance of a destination.

"Go!" Sadie's voice followed him.

She might have said, "Get our girl and bring her back," but Hugo's mind was otherwise engaged with thoughts of Amber.

He'd made the mistake of thinking he was a man who had it all, but he wasn't even close.

Not without her. She was his counterweight. The yin to his yang. The uptight hippy to his laid-back royalty.

And he loved her. Deeply. Ferociously.

Not because of the baby. Her child, their child, was important. But right now, it was only a dream. A fairy tale he hoped would come true.

Amber was his reality.

With that as his touchstone, Hugo hit the bottom of the stairs, sweat sliding down his face, his heart like a runaway horse, and burst out into the light.

* * *

Amber sat in the back of the town car, Ned sitting in the footwell, Prospero in the back seat with her, a strange smile playing around his eyes.

They came out through a copse that hung over the bumpy country road and the palace came into view.

"Are you sure about this, Your Highness?" Prospero asked.

She shot him a look. "You're the one who said Hugo sounded strange."

"Very strange."

"If you're pulling my leg and I drive up there and find him sitting in his office surrounded by lackeys, I will find out if I have the authority to send you to—"

"Siberia?"

She'd been about to say Mongolia, but Siberia was close enough.

Staying in the shack, sleeping, reading books that weren't about princesses—mostly about what to do when you were expecting—and snuggling with Ned and talking to Sunflower and Johnno on the phone had been exactly what she'd needed.

Too long feeling like a car in need of a service—clunky and misfiring—she was now a finely tuned machine. Waking at six, yoga by sunrise, nap at three, bed by nine. Eating clean, drinking water like it was going out of fashion. She was the picture of hippy health.

And she couldn't remember ever feeling so miserable in her life.

The truth was, when she'd heard Prospero answer the phone she'd known it was Hugo on the other end. She so wanted to hear his voice, to make sure he was all right, perhaps even to fight with him a little so as to get her blood sparking again, it was a miracle she didn't tear the phone from Prospero's grip.

When Prospero had murmured something about the Prince sounding strange on the phone she'd practically grabbed him by the collar and dragged him to the car.

She might not have figured out what she'd gone to the shack to figure out, but she had discovered something. That she missed him. Missed his humour, his work ethic, the way he looked at her as if he'd never seen anything quite like her.

And that in the grip of old fears, she may have judged him too harshly.

The only way to figure out what they were to one another was to figure it out together.

Minutes later, the car pulled through the front gates of the Palace of Vallemont. It hooked around the back, heading towards one of the huge garages.

Prospero helped her out of the car.

She stretched her legs, looking into the garden

leading to the forest. The one she could see from her balcony, where she'd seen Hugo wash Ned with his own bare hands and whatever methods she'd used to deny her feelings had truly dissolved away.

Hang on a second. What was that? A big white tent-type structure had been put up on the lawn since the last time she was there.

Curious, she took a few steps that way, only to see Hugo striding inside the thing as if his life depended on it, wearing what looked like an old knit jumper, dirty jeans and gumboots. His nose was pink, his beanie ragged.

He looked like a right royal mess. And she loved him more than anything.

Maybe that was what she'd figured out in the shack: that she could love their little family enough for the both of them.

Then suddenly Hugo was back at the entrance, what looked like a pile of weeds in his hand.

She saw the moment he clocked her.

She wasn't sure how he might react, whether she would get warm Hugo, or cool Hugo, or a whole new beast. Perhaps the Hugo she had left in the lurch.

But then he mouthed her name and soon he was running.

And she was running too, her bag dumped by the car.

And then she was in his arms, wrapped tightly.

His face was buried in her neck, tears sliding down her face.

And then they were kissing as if they hadn't seen one another in weeks rather than days. And maybe they hadn't. Not really.

Amber slowly slid down Hugo's body, her feet touching the ground before their lips came apart. Then she blinked up into his eyes and knew. Something had happened to him in their separation as it had happened to her. Something magical.

"Hi," she said.

"Hi to you too."

His gaze slid past her shoulder to where Prospero stood on edge of the hill. Once Hugo gave him the all-clear he slipped into the shadows and was gone.

"What are you doing here, *miele*? I was just about to come and find you. If I'd known you hadn't fled to the other side of the world I'd have been there sooner. I'd have been there every day and night. Doing whatever it took to convince you that I want you here. With me. I want you at my side. In my bed. In my damn apartment. Or I'll move into your sparkly pink monstrosity if that's what it will take to show you I mean it."

She laughed at the words pouring from his lips. "Slow down before you hurt yourself."

"Too late," he said, reaching up to swipe her

hair from her face. Then, realising he still gripped the weeds, he stepped back and held them out to her. "These were for you."

"Thank you...?"

"They're lavender seedlings. Not yet flowering, clearly. But with the bees at play we should see a good crop that we can plant along this patch of grass so you can see them from our window. *Our* window."

"Hugo?"

"Hmmm."

"I have no idea what you are talking about." Not that it mattered. He could have been talking wheat prices and sheep farming for all she cared. For he had his hand in hers, and the look in his eye made her feel faint.

"Right," he said. "Of course. Come on."

He took her by the hand and dragged her down the grassy slope. Up close, the tent was huge. Taller than a tree and half the size of a soccer field. With a half-smile, Hugo opened the flap with a flourish.

What hit her first was the heat. It was a hothouse. As humid and warm as an Australian spring. To go with it, a small forest had been planted in her absence. Wattle trees and banksia, liquidambar saplings and pots and pots of lavender. And buzzing around the lot were tiny little stingless Australian bees.

"Hugo, what have you done?"

"It's not finished yet. Not by a long shot. But it's a start."

"A start of what? Turning this into Australia?"

"Just this patch. Just for you. I realised that I had torn you out of your natural environment and stuck you in a cage when I should have been nurturing you. Nurturing *us*. I somehow thought that if I built this, a little patch of home, it might be enough to tempt you back."

He took her by the shoulders and moved her.

In the far corner, two huge trees had been transplanted into the soil. Mature gum trees, no less. And between them swung a hammock.

Seeing it, Amber burst into tears.

Hugo spun her around, stooped to look into her eyes. "Oh, hell, Amber."

Hands on her shoulders, he hustled her out of the hothouse and into the fresh air. "I'm sorry. Has it made you homesick? I can take it down. I'm not good at this kind of thing."

"What kind of thing is that exactly?" she asked, knowing but wanting to hear him say it.

"Romance."

She burst into laughter. "You toss a priceless family heirloom at me as if it's a trinket." She wangled her hand at him to prove her point. "And you romance me with a hammock."

He felt for her hand, held it up to the light. "You're wearing the ring."

"Of course I'm wearing your ring, Hugo. I've never taken it off. You could have given me the pull ring from a soda can and I'd still be wearing it. Because you gave it to me."

She grabbed him by the front of the jumper, a light glinted in his eye and he smiled. It was enough to push her over her last great hurdle. And once she leapt she felt as if she could fly.

"I don't need romance, you great big lug. Or crown jewels. Or a staff. Or a huge apartment of my own. I just need you." She breathed in, not sure if the words would come. But then it was as easy as breathing out as she said, "I love you, Hugo. I love you so much I'm willing to put up with your odd bodyguard and your family's strange obsession with the colour pink. I don't need romance, Hugo, I just need you." And with that she pulled him in and kissed him until she was about to faint. Then just a little more because it felt that good.

When she pulled back she was woozy with lust, and lack of oxygen, so she wasn't quick enough to stop him when he sank to one knee. "Get up."

"No."

She looked around to see a couple of gardeners watching from the hedgerow. A band of maids had congregated by the laundry door. Marguerite stood watching from a balcony on the first floor, her hand to her mouth. From that distance, Amber could have sworn she saw tears. "Hugo, please. I don't need this."

"Amber Hartley Giordano."

Amber looked down at the Prince and the rest of the world faded to nothing. "Yes, Hugo?"

"You may think you don't need romance, but I'm afraid that you live in a palace now, and you are married to a prince. Romance will from this point on be a given. Because I am besotted. Fuelled by desire. I am crazy in love. With you. I'd convinced myself it was dangerous to love that hard. But the only danger was the possibility of losing you because I never let you know it."

Amber was speechless, overwhelmed and so happy her cheeks hurt from smiling. "Right back at you. Now please get up."

"Not until you agree to marry me."

"I already did."

"Again. In front of your friends and mine. In front of God and country. And the world."

He was too big for her to lift, and too stubborn to convince, so she sank to her knees as well. "Okay."

"Really?"

"Why not?"

He leaned down, kissed her gently. Pulled back. "You like the hammock?"

"I love the hammock. I can't wait till everyone's asleep and we can sneak out to the hammock and…" She leaned in, whispering her intentions in his ear.

"I can order them all to bed now, you know. I have that power."

"No, you don't."

"You're right, I don't. So later, then?"

"It's a date."

"A date. I don't believe we ever had one of those."

"Now seems like a fine time to start."

Two weeks later, Marguerite got the wedding she wanted. Hugo had insisted on a no-camera policy inside the chapel, but the guest list was extensive and the decor extravagant.

The bride wore pink, because it was tradition. She was even beginning to get used to the colour.

"You look edible."

Amber turned to find Hugo leaning in the doorway of the anteroom in which she was getting ready. Then Sadie leapt in between them, waving her arms like a mad thing.

"Get out! It's bad luck to see her before the wedding. Your mother's family was dripping in bad luck, remember, Your Highness. Should you really risk it?"

"Bad things happen," said Hugo. "We do what we must to fend them off. Protecting those we love. It's been the way of things since the time of cavemen. Fending off sabre-tooth tigers with big sticks. It's not all that different now. Besides, if you don't remember, we're already married. You were even there."

"Oh, right. So this is all…"

"For the good of the country."

"I've heard that before."

"Mmm," said Hugo before taking Sadie by the hips, spinning her and pushing her forcibly out of the door, which he locked behind her.

Amber simply kept on pinning a silk peony rose she had unpicked from her coronation gown into her hair.

He moved in behind her, placing his hands on her gently rounded belly and kissing her on the neck. "Morning, wife."

"Morning, husband."

"Nearly ready?"

"I was born ready."

"Yes, you were. I had a quick look at the crowd."

"And?"

"Hell of a crowd. Nearly as big as my last wedding."

She caught his eye in the mirror. "Funny man."

"I try. When you get out there don't forget to check out the first few rows."

"Why?"

"Just do it."

"Tell me why. Right now."

"Fine, but only because I can't resist you when you get all bossy on me. On the right we have my mother sitting in a better position than Marguerite and clearly loving it, while my aunt looks as pleased as if she sucked a lemon. And on the left of the chapel, in a sea of hemp formal wear, half of Serenity."

"What? How?"

"We flew them in on a chartered plane yesterday." Hugo held out both hands, smug as all get-out.

"You really are a powerful man."

"Handsome too, don't forget."

"So handsome," she said, her finger climbing up the front of his shirt before popping a button.

"Oops," Hugo said with a smile.

When his hand went to her back, unzipping her simple, floaty dress in one fell swoop, there was no time for "oops". For soon they were both undressed, their wedding clothes strewn on the floor, and both glad Hugo had locked the door.

When the wedding start time came and went, the crowd did wonder if they might be about to see another exciting non-wedding at the Palace of Vallemont. But when the bride and groom took one another down the aisle fifteen minutes later, it was clear to everyone present how smitten they both were.

And that a new day was dawning in the story of Vallemont.

EPILOGUE

"Aaaargh!"

The midwife gave Hugo a look.

"Sorry," he whispered. "I stubbed my toe."

Amber rolled her eyes. Which was quite a feat, considering she'd been in labour for six hours and didn't feel as if she had the energy to breathe, much less express sarcasm in any meaningful way.

"I never imagined His Highness to be so precious," the midwife said to Amber, loud enough for Hugo to hear.

"It's a new thing. He seems to think I am made of glass and, in response, his tiptoeing skills have become excellent."

The tingle in the base of her spine, and the encroaching red at the edges of her mind, heralded another contraction. Amber closed her eyes, breathed gently and counted to fifteen. When she reached the peak, she rode the relief counting back down to one.

The midwife pottered about, doing her wonderful, calming, capable, midwifey things, and, after a glance to be sure Amber was back, said, "So how did you two lovebirds meet?"

"You really don't know?"

The midwife shot her a look.

"Of course you know. You're just trying to distract me. It's a long and winding tale," said Amber.

"We have time," she said, glancing at her watch as she checked Amber's pulse. "Not much, but a little."

Hugo caught Amber's eye, panic swirling about the hazel depths. "How little?" he asked.

"That's up to the little Prince or Princess." The midwife threw him a smile. Before patting Amber on the hand. "You are doing great. Textbook."

"Hear that?" Amber said as another wave of pain ripped through her body. "I'm a natural."

"You are perfect."

The midwife scoffed. "Don't ever let him forget he said that."

Amber smiled as the pain ebbed.

At which point the midwife had a look and a feel. She held Amber's eyes. "Are you ready to have a baby, Your Highness?"

Amber nodded. After months of nausea, followed by months of baby bliss, then months of swollen feet and arguments with Marguerite as to the nursery colours, she was so ready to have a baby, this man's baby, she could barely hold herself together. Her joy was such she felt as if she might split into a thousand pieces.

Hugo, on the other hand, groaned as if he might not last.

"Perhaps His Highness could go to the desk, track down another heat pack?"

Hugo wagged a finger at the midwife. "Not happening. I've spoken to other fathers. I know the tricks you lot pull when you think we're not handling things. I am fine. I will not miss the birth of my daughter."

"Or son," Amber said through gritted teeth as she hit thirteen, fourteen, fifteen, sixteen, seventeen... The pain was different now—bigger, broader—and she gripped the edges of her subconscious as it tried to disintegrate. Thankfully her body seemed to know what to do even if her mind was shutting up shop; taking over, bearing down.

And then...relief.

"That's right," said Hugo, suddenly at her side, holding her hand. Though his knuckles looked strangely white—bloodless, in fact...because she was squeezing the life out of them.

Amber let go. Or tried. But Hugo wrapped his hand around hers.

"We had a summer affair in a beautiful little country town in Australia," he said, eyes on hers. "Which ended when she kicked me out of her bed for no reason whatsoever."

Amber tried to open her mouth to disagree,

but reality had taken a hike. Her head was full of stars. Her body felt as if it was floating above the bed, no doubt trying to escape the pain.

Hugo's deep voice was like a balm. "After that we got to know one another and discovered we actually liked one another. Knowing then I'd never met a woman of her like—fierce and fearless, loyal and lovely, bright and bold—I found myself terrified I'd screw up the best thing that had ever happened to me, so I did my very best to screw it up just to make sure."

Amber heard it all through the spangled depths of her brain as she came out of her next contraction. The urge to scream was stoppered by the stronger need to hear Hugo's words.

"The rest was pretty textbook. We found out we were pregnant; we got married; I was crowned; she became a princess; she left me; I willed her back." With his spare hand, Hugo pushed damp hair from Amber's cheek, tucking it behind her ear. "And somewhere in there we fell in love."

"And then…?"

"I'm hoping the 'and then' will be born pretty soon. Healthy, whole, and as beautiful as my wife."

Amber felt a tear running down her cheek even as she fell into the mental abyss that was birthing a baby. No matter how much she wanted to look into Hugo's eyes, to tell him how deeply she loved him, her eyes closed, her breaths came hard and fast and she dug deep, knowing she'd need every bit of energy she had to get through this.

The midwife's voice came as if down a tunnel. "I like it. Very modern. Though I'm not sure there's a greetings card that covers it."

"I'd expect not."

"Your Highness? Amber?"

Amber opened her eyes to see a team of people now milling about the room. The midwife clicked her fingers to make sure Amber was looking into her eyes. "The baby's head is clear, Amber. One more good push and your baby will be born."

Amber looked to Hugo. A matching tear left a track down his cheek too.

"You ready for this?" she asked. "For all of this? For us?

Hugo's smile was slow. Warm. Genuine. "I was born ready."

And somehow, Amber found the strength to laugh.

Half an hour later, after weighing and measuring and the most fundamentally soulful moments of Hugo's life to date—watching his wife smile and coo and glow as she enjoyed skin-to-skin time with her child—Hugo held a bundle of snuggly swaddled baby in his arms.

He kept his voice low so as not to wake Amber

as he said, "I know I said your mother was perfect, and she'll never let me forget it, but I do believe I was jumping the gun. You," he said, looking down at the face of his baby daughter, "you are perfect."

Amber stirred and settled. Hugo knew she'd wake up grumpy, having fallen asleep and missed this, but after witnessing what her body had put her through for the past several hours Hugo did not wake her. Not just yet.

His daughter was sleeping too, still too squishy from her own recent ordeal to look much like her mother, but he could see the potential in the lashes brushing her cheeks, in the shape of her chin, the tuft of fair hair. Lucky girl.

Give her a day to grow into her new world and Princess Lucinda Sadie Sunflower Giordano would be the most beautiful child that ever was. And the most loved.

Princess or no princess, she had two parents who wanted her and adored one another so very, very much. Add an adoring dog, a dozen already besotted honorary aunts and uncles on the other side of the world, and a mini-hammock he had secretly hung in the hothouse as a surprise and Hugo knew this kid was as lucky as they came.

If Hugo had his way in the next session of parliament—and if that was what she wanted to be—he was looking upon the face of the girl who could one day become the first Sovereign Princess of Vallemont.

Shifting gently on his chair, instinctively mindful that not waking the baby was going to be a big deal, he leaned towards his wife and kissed her on the cheek. Then the edge of her mouth. Then her lips.

Her eyes fluttered open in surprise, before softening as she kissed him back.

"Lucy?" she said.

And Hugo shifted so she could see her baby.

"She has your nose."

"Poor kid."

"I love your nose," Amber said with a frown, so loyal to those she cared for she wouldn't even let him make a joke about himself.

"As you should. For it is the nose of princes and princesses."

"It's the nose of Hugo; that's all I care about."

"You did good, kiddo."

"I did, didn't I?"

"Did it hurt as much as it seemed?"

"More."

"Want to do it again?"

"As soon as humanly possible."

Hugo gave Amber a nudge and with a wince she scooched over so that the entire family could fit on the big hospital bed.

"But first, I want to talk to you about the

nurses. I got talking to one when you were on a phone call earlier, about their working conditions. I believe we can do better for them. Job share for those who are keen. Add a crèche. I want to know more about mandatory breaks. I might even have offered to represent them…"

Hugo laughed. "Please tell me you're not about to call me out in front of parliament."

"Do the right thing and I won't have to."

"It's a deal."

Amber snuggled deeper into the bed, wincing again as she moved, but looking happier than he had ever seen her. "I'm going to like this job, aren't I?"

"Told you so. Vallemont has no idea how lucky it is to have you on its side, *miele*."

"Right back at you, My Highness."

With his daughter secure in his arms, Hugo leaned down and kissed his Princess, his wife, his partner, his conscience, his love. And the rogue Prince of Vallemont had finally found his way home.

* * * * *